THE SAGE HEN

To Orville from Clara.
Dec. 1938

THE SAGE HEN

By F. R. BUCKLEY

A. L. BURT COMPANY
Publishers   New York

Published by arrangement with The Bobbs-Merrill Company
Printed in U. S. A.

Copyright (serially), 1923
By Street & Smith Corporation

Copyright, 1925
By The Bobbs-Merrill Company

Printed in the United States of America

To
JOAN-NELL
In memory of the dark days at the Circle B

THE SAGE HEN

THE SAGE HEN

CHAPTER I

EMERGING from a light slumber on the porch of his International Emporium & Sheriff's Office, Mr. William Garfield half opened his eyes on the spectacle of a pair of boots, resting, like his own boot and peg-leg, on the sun-bleached porch railing.

Immediately, closing his lids with the firmness of panic, he made desperate attempts to return to the land of dreams.

It was a spring afternoon of the sunniest and warmest, into which, a brown cigarette sparkling amid his straggling gray whiskers, the sheriff of Three Pines had ambled forth after lunch, with the general idea of recuperating from a morning spent assuring himself that the stock of his store was much the same as it had been three months before, and that the vital statistics and the freight receipts were still in their usual condition of hopeless confusion. The air was bland and fragrant with the subtle scent of fresh-growing grass and opening buds, to which, with the piquant effect of salt in a cantaloupe, there was added the tang of alkali dust. Over along the Rio Grande, the violet-tinted foothills were endowed with a soft tremulousness as the winter-soaked soil of the plain gave back its stored moisture to the soft blue sky. It was Mr. Garfield's seventy-sixth consecutive spring; he surveyed its gracious signs long and longingly before— Though it is really inexact to say he went to sleep. Rather, the body confessed itself weak; and, retiring, permitted the youthful spirit an hour of wandering in the past.

But when this permission had been accorded, the permissionaire had been alone. The appearance of a pair of boots before his waking gaze meant that somebody had occupied the other porch chair while he—while he had been gone. Boots in that particularly easy, familiar pose on the porch rail seemed to indicate that the newcomer was Jake Henson; the presence of Jake Henson meant—trouble.

Mr. Garfield was not in a trouble-seeking mood.

THE SAGE HEN

How much more pleasant to slip warmly back—knowing quite well that the slippage was a disgraceful dereliction of—no, not duty; Hurst County was not Mr. Garfield's bailiwick; let 'em kill each other if they—though that girl, there, just as Jake said—Well, anyway. Slip back to that day in the spring of 'sixty-eight, when a lean young man with two meat legs, and without a vestige either of gray whisker on his face or of general store on his back—had stuffed a hundred dollars of pay (in the form of a ring)—down into the recesses of his breast-pocket, and started over from Laredo to call on Miss Lily James! Sunshine, and a scented breeze, prairie flowers pretty nigh up to the horse's belly; and not a single darn square-toed riding boot—meaning trouble—in sight.

Never mind about boots. . . . And then, getting to Lily's, just as the sun was painting the sky red and gold, and the hills royal purple, and the grass lands that queer sort of gray-pink. . . .

Like the interlocking device of a block-signal, protesting against the carelessness of the man at the switch, the boots bobbed up again into Mr. Garfield's swooning consciousness.

THE SAGE HEN

Boots. . . .

Jake Henson's boots. . . .

With the red Lone Star worked on 'em. . . .

One of the aged eyes flew open, followed closely by the other. That was the disturbing element, then . . . these boots lacked the red stars. Jake must have got a new—but, no. Come to notice, the trousers tucked into their tops were of gray whipcord instead of khaki, and—

The sheriff permitted his tilted chair to come down on all fours with a crash, and his now fully-opened eyes to travel past the trousers to the gun belt, up the shirt, past the blue silk neckcloth, to the face of the semi-recumbent man beside him.

It was the face of a perfect stranger.

Seeing which, Mr. Garfield started violently, and became wide awake.

"Hello!" he greeted rather vaguely.

"Hello," said the young man in the chair.

He *was* a young man, old Bill Garfield decided; and yet somehow he seemed a great deal older than he looked; a most unsettling state of affairs. It was impossible, by any stretching of the ordinary standards, to judge him a day over twenty-eight;

THE SAGE HEN

and yet there was something about him, as he lay there, ankles crossed, a cigarette drifting its smoke over the back of a lean brown hand, that filled an observer's mind with the impossible word "forty."

Mr. Garfield moved a gnarled old hand in search of his tobacco.

Instantly, the half-closed eyes of the man before him snapped wide open, and the hand which had been holding the cigarette dropped it, and flew up to scratch its owner's chin. If a desire for tobacco from a breast pocket may cover a reach for an armpit holster, an itch in the hypogastric region may likewise bring a hand to the position for a quick drop to the belt.

It was as the two men stared at each other that Mr. Garfield solved the problem of the other's age. The eyes made the difference. The chin scratcher's face was young; but somehow, he seemed to have stolen his grandfather's eyes.

"You'll know me again, I hope?"

The sheriff, with a deft sweep of his hand down the front of his right thigh, rolled paper and tobacco into a cylinder, and nicked a match into flame with an expert thumb-nail.

"Know you," he answered, puffing, "already—m'pf. Darn! Got a lucifer?"

The young man made no move to oblige; though, slowly, he lowered his feet from the porch railing and sat upright. The hand which had been at his chin now dropped by imperceptible degrees and toyed with a shirt button six inches nearer his belt.

"By which I don't mean to say," remarked old Bill Garfield casually, "that I know your name, height, weight and criminal record. In fact, I don't."

The hand dropped, according to its program, one button lower, but the muscles that had ridged its back, relaxed.

"What do you know, then?"

"Why," said the sheriff of Three Pines, "I'll tell you. First, I know you've come over the Rio Grande, because there's mud on your boots made of water and red sand from Pueblo Indio. See? For another thing, you roll your butts with a maize wrappin'—and if you don't mind, I'll take a light from this one you dropped. M'pf, m'pf. Ah! Well, then again, I can see by your clothes that you've bin drawin' down a good deal more than

THE SAGE HEN

forty a month an' found; an' you're posted on the fact that I'm a peace officer; an' you're nervous with your guns. There's other signs; but with just these, you won't blame me for hazardin' a shrewd guess that you're bound over the hills to Hurst County, and that if I said 'Sage Hen' suddenly, you'd jump."

The subject of the analysis said nothing.

"Besides," said Mr. Garfield, after a considerable period of examining his companion's face, "I've been expecting you."

"You've got a letter for me."

"I *had* a letter for you—if you're John Arnold," said the sheriff, examining the red tip of his cigarette. "And that kind of brings me to the point I've been wondering whether I should come to or not. I'm not generally afflicted with any great love for gunmen, but these circumstances are a bit peculiar. When a letter's left with me, I feel kind of responsible. Besides, though you ain't much on conversation and have habits I deplore, I rather take to you, Arnold. So I'm going to give you a chunk of valuable advice. You put your hoss in my corral when you got here?"

THE SAGE HEN

John Arnold nodded.

Mr. Garfield drew and examined a portentous silver watch.

"It's now ten minutes to three," he remarked, "and here's the advice. Get your horse out again, and by three, be a good long way from here."

"Why?"

Old Bill leaned back and took a long reflective drag at his cigarette.

"Well, I'll tell you," he said, "and here's why I'll tell you. Hurst County's no business of mine, understand; if they want to have cattle wars over there, an' their sheriff's agreeable, that's up to them. But—here's the first thing I'm tellin' you—this war's so darn lopsided it kind of makes me sick to see it gettin' any lopsideder, an' I think it will you, when you know about it. You're one of the International Beef Concern's men—oh, that's all right; only I mean, perhaps you haven't got the dope straight. You know it's a billion-dollar company an' all that; but do you know who it's fightin' in Hurst County, an' has been for the last year? It was fightin' old Daddy Bruce an' his son at first— an' it killed them both. But do you know who it's fightin' now? Do you know who's stickin' to the

Circle R, an' fightin' the whole works now? One girl! Joan Bruce. Yeah—you've heard of her— The 'Sage Hen.' Well—for the first thing, I don't like to see any more men linin' up against her."

There was a dull flush in Arnold's cheeks; but he said nothing. The hand, however, which had rested so near his right gun butt, now traveled away in quest of the makings.

"It'd look better," suggested Mr. Garfield after a pause, "if you'd sling your hook after bein' told that, than after what I'm goin' to tell you next."

"Thanks," said the young man—and did not move.

"Well, then, here's the second thing. There was a letter left here for you yesterday by a guy named Soper. I took it, an' said I'd give it to you. I can't, because I ain't got it. An' I ain't got it because it was taken away from me by a friend of Joan Bruce's, who'd recognized Soper as one of the beef concern's bright and particular woman-fighters. He read that letter, Dave Grant did, right then and there, coverin' me with a gun while he did it; an' then he asked me to keep you here till three o'clock. It's—five minutes to, right now."

Mr. Arnold smiled.

THE SAGE HEN

"Is this Dave Grant from Corpus Christi?" he asked, with a strange new briskness.

"It's no Dave Grant you're ever likely to have met," said the sheriff warningly, "so don't count on it. This guy met Joan Bruce while she was at college in the East, before her dad and brother were murdered; an' when she said she was comin' West to take up the fight, he followed—to look after her. Well—you couldn't get away now, so I'll tell you what you're in for. He's in love with her, of course, which won't make him like you any at all; an' she won't let him marry her an' stand in on the fight; an' just lately, she's given him the razz entirely, for hangin' around an' doin' this guerrilla warfare for her. See? She says she won't break the law, like the I. B. T.'s doin'. She'll just defend herself. Well, he knows better than that; so she's— That'll make him feel fine, for another thing. I think you could run for it, even now."

"That'd be rather undignified, don't you think?" asked Arnold.

"If that's what you're after," Mr. Garfield said slowly, "there's nothing so dignified as a really good funeral."

THE SAGE HEN

The young man laughed.

"I begin," he said, throwing one leg over the arm of his chair, "to take to you in turn, Mr. Garfield. Is that the chap over there, by any chance?"

"Yes!"

Arnold let smoke dribble slowly out of his nostrils.

"Good shoulders," he remarked casually.

"Intercollegiate heavyweight champion last year," remarked Mr. Garfield with equal nonchalance.

CHAPTER II

THERE was silence on the porch until the flying pony which bore Dave Grant had approached within a hundred yards. Then John Arnold threw away his cigarette, blew out a last wreath of smoke, unbuckled and dropped his gun belt, and stretched extensively.

"It's a pity," he said, "that love should have such an effect in balling everything up, Mr. Garfield. I'm sorry about this."

He took his stand at the head of the steps, arms folded, the sunshine blazing full into his long brown face, just at the moment when Grant, his right hand on a gun butt, hurled himself off his pony.

"Is your name John Arnold?" asked the man from the East.

"Yes. I thought you might prefer fists."

Dave Grant's face, still sufficiently new to the dry hot winds, the hard water, and the driving sand of the county, to seem boyishly fresh when contrasted with that of his adversary, twisted into a grin; a furious grin; a grin like that of a hungry wolf whose mouth drips with desire for blood.

Mr. Garfield, isolated alike by years and porch railing, reflected that the custom of applying the wolf simile to bad men only was really quite unjust. Given similar emotions, the best of men can look quite as wolfish as the worst. The praiseworthy cause of the emotion, the admirable object of it, failing to remove from the expression one atom of the unrestrained ferocity, the visible delight in the red carnival ahead.

"You thought so, did you?" asked Dave Grant through his teeth. "All right, then! Come on down."

There was a moment's pause.

"Or do you want me to fetch you?"

"Quite sure," asked Arnold, coming down one step, as Grant dropped his gun belt in the dust, "that there's no questions you want to ask, or anything, before we begin?"

"I've had all I wanted answered by that letter," snarled Grant. "Come on, you hired thug, you!"

Arnold's arms unfolded with a spasmodic movement. But his voice, as he spoke from the next step lower, was cold and level.

"Any questions you want to ask—about that letter?" he said, with a strange reluctance, as if he spoke the words against his better judgment.

"No!"

"All right, then."

As the stranger's foot touched the loose alkali dust of the level, before, it seemed, he could have had time to raise the arms which had hung limply at his sides, Dave Grant was upon him with a terrible rush. Two hollow thumps sounded as the attacker's fists rang against Arnold's ribs with force enough, it seemed, to knock the breath out of an elephant; then the man from across the Rio Grande blocked a terrible left for the jaw, countered and sprang forward.

The next instant, the combat was at its height; two giants, in a cloud of dust, colored red by the dying sun, standing toe to toe, dealing blows that seemed to jar the very ground.

"My God above!" whispered old Bill Garfield in his chair.

They were very evenly matched in point of weight

and reach; and, to any one but a connoisseur of battles—a practising connoisseur, who abhorred ringside seats—Grant's more clear-cut science might have seemed to equalize a certain concentration and solidity which one somehow associated with the other man; but the aged gentleman on the porch was not deceived. With narrowed eyes, he watched the younger man break a clinch with practised heave of the shoulders, cover his get-away with just the right punch, and return to the attack with a perfectly-timed series of straight drives which sent Arnold to his knees; he watched Arnold rise, rocking under a cruel pounding; he watched him, on his feet again, offer his face as a target while, with chin down and arms over the mark, he regained his breath. And, even before the stranger started to take his turn at the attack, Mr. Garfield's right hand was betting his left five to one in favor of Arnold. In seventy-odd years of fairly continuous fighting, one learns that there is only one thing about a fighter to bet on, and that is his spirit.

"Ah!" said the sheriff suddenly.

With every trick known to the coaches, Grant was blocking the attack; but, slowly, into his eyes there was creeping a look of apprehension. The attacker should have been tired by now—should have given a split-second's opportunity for a change of lead, but he was not tired; he bored in with the terrible persistence of a steam engine; and, since an irresistible force and an immovable obstacle can not co-exist, Dave Grant began to weaken. When old Bill Garfield exclaimed, Arnold's fist, flashing toward the jaw, had touched its objective before it was brushed aside by a guard which came just in time. A drive for the solar plexus, diverted by the narrowest margin to the lower ribs, shook Grant to his toes.

Inevitably, his attempt to stop the uppercut which, in the same instant, sought his jaw again, was long behind the times. He craned his head on one side, and the iron-hard fist missed the deadly nerve terminal at the point; but he was off his balance, and the mere impact on the jaw-bone was enough to spill him, without the additional punch which thudded home under his eye.

Dave Grant fell on all fours.

"Enough?" gasped his adversary, bending over him.

THE SAGE HEN

The fallen man shook his head dazedly, and tried to draw one foot under him.

"If you're willing to listen to me," came Arnold's breathless whisper, "I'm willin'—talk to you."

Grant's attempt to rise was suddenly successful. Still staggering, he got to his feet and stepped forward until his shoulder touched Arnold's.

"I—listen to no thugs," he muttered. "I don't —talk—to skunks."

"Then you'd better haul off and recover a bit," his opponent told him.

"Recover hell!" shouted Grant, and, on the word, his powerful shoulders gave the beginning of the droop which precedes an uppercut.

Instantly, something seemed to explode inside his head, Arnold's face before him, its lips suddenly tightened with effort, to turn a fiery red and to vomit stars; and the sunshine to be eclipsed by an inky pall. Dimly, as from a great distance, he heard a voice—Arnold's voice—saying something about some old trick that hadn't worked since 1890, strangely, as if his body were wrapped in many layers of cotton-wool, he felt himself seized, picked up, carried and laid down; and—

Then, with most contradictory consciousnesses that he was awake, that he was asleep, that he was in acute pain, and that he was perfectly comfortable, the intercollegiate champion permitted his remaining senses to slide from him.

"He's young and inexperienced," said John Arnold, over his body, "that's all, Mis'—Garfield. Oughta—listened—me—first; oughn'—punched—like that at end."

"He's a treacherous young dog!" roared old Bill Garfield. "If you hadn't got to his plexus before he reached your jaw, he'd have half killed you when you hadn't your hands up."

Arnold refreshed himself with several deep breaths, and carefully felt the environs of his left eye.

"You don't want to figure him too harsh, Mr. Garfield," he said. "See, he reckoned I was just like vermin—get me out of the way, no matter how. You don't feel—'bliged—woof!—to shoot gophers only when they're running. Put up fine fight; but—he's young. I heard he was—across the Rio."

"I'll bet he's less'n two years younger than you," growled the sheriff.

THE SAGE HEN

"But look how fast I've lived! By the way, I wonder if our young friend has that letter of mine on him. M-m-m. Yes. Here it is."

"I hear," said Mr. Garfield gravely, "that the years pass mighty slow—in jail."

The man addressed did not look up from his reading.

"They pass mighty fast when you're running away from it," he murmured.

The sheriff of Three Pines scratched his chin.

"When you're quite done with the literature," he said diffidently, "I'd like a word with you. H'm."

"Official?"

"Paternal."

Arnold folded the letter and stuck it in his pocket. Then he lifted Grant's eyelid with his thumb, examined the insensitive eyeball underneath, remarked that there was nothing to be done except what nature would attend to; and then seated himself again.

"Shoot!" he invited, smiling.

Mr. Garfield seemed to think it wasn't quite so simple as all that. Balancing himself on the porch railing, and confining his gaze to the cigarette he was rolling, he coughed twice before he began, and then said nothing more sensational than that he wished he knew what Arnold had been going to tell his late foe.

"I'm glad you don't," said the victor. "I'm glad he doesn't, too. I was a fool to think of saying anything. Too soft, I guess. Nothing—nothing of importance, anyhow."

"I thought maybe," said the old man, "that you wanted to tell him you weren't really an International Beef Concern gunman. Sorry for the word, but I don't use no thesaurus."

"Well, I am."

The blunt avowal startled Mr. Garfield.

"You don't seem quite the type to me," he protested, rather weakly.

John Arnold heaved himself out of his chair, and towered over the old sheriff, a tense column of man, bloody and ragged.

"Look here," he said, "I like you, Mr. Garfield. You're all right; and you don't come in on this officially. I—"

"Joan Bruce's sort of a friend of mine," said old Bill in passing.

"Well, anyway, I'm not going to sail under any

false colors with you. I'm not asking for any favors from any man. I'm what I am—yes, and what I have been, too."

"What I wanted to talk about," said Mr. Garfield, "is more what you will be."

Arnold gave a short laugh.

"As for that, I'm hired by the I. B. C., I'm paid by the I. B. C., and—I'm going to be hired and paid by the I. B. C. Not much to talk about."

"Will you let me talk about it for two minutes?" asked old Bill Garfield, pulling out the watch. "Without interruptions?"

Arnold nodded and returned to his chair. Mr. Garfield, with a considerable show of exactitude, waited until the second hand of his chronometer was at 60, and then, with a bland disregard for the terms of the covenant, slipped the clanking turnip back into his fob-pocket.

"Exhibit A," he said, pointing to the limp figure of Dave Grant. Then he waved his arm toward the dusk-shrouded hills marking the boundaries of Hurst County. "Exhibit B—your enemy, the Sage Hen. She called herself that when she came down here to bury her father, and to find her brother not only dead, but missin'. They're a rough lot—I mean, you're a rough lot, you I. B. C. folks. Dunno what they—what you did with young Bruce's body. An I. B. C. man boasted of havin' shot him and then cut his throat as he lay wounded; an' since the sheriff over there's an I. B. C. man, too, like the judges and the juries—I went over after that beef murderer myself. But he'd gone. . . . Where was I? Oh, yes. The Sage Hen. See, her relatives in the East came after her, and reminded her of what she was missin', in the way of concerts, an' theaters, an' marriages, an' all that; an' she told 'em that her job was what her father'd left unfinished, and her place was right here, an' that she was goin' to be a sage hen for the rest of her life, if necessary. There was a lot of people friendly to her then—they've been chased out of the county since. There was a raft of punchers left from her dad's time—they've been shot, an' jailed, an' one thing and another, most of 'em. There was a railway she could ship stock out on, an' get enough to pay her bills with—the I. B. C. owns it now. An' still she sticks to the Circle R, and won't sell out at the price they offer—ten cents an acre, by the way."

THE SAGE HEN

Mr. Garfield's cigarette had come unstuck. He licked it carefully.

"So," he added, "they're goin' to make a real big drive, an' just plain throw her off her land."

To the naked eye, the cigarette seemed securely glued now; but the sheriff created an interesting pause by licking it again.

"That," he said, "will be your job, Arnold."

"Finished?" asked the man in the chair, a queer tremor shaking his voice.

Mr. Garfield puffed and nodded.

His disciple arose.

Unhurriedly, deliberately, he picked up the gun belt he had dropped on the porch, buckled it about him, and, by the sense of touch, returned his scrambled clothes to the semblance of normality. His hat had fallen at the foot of the porch steps; he picked it up, wincing a little as he bent over, dusted it on his ragged sleeve, and replaced it on his head dented in the manner which, being typical of Texas, is known as the Montana poke. From just inside the International Emporium proper, he lifted out his saddle and a Winchester .30-.30 whose stock displayed the sheen only obtainable with

23

water, heat, sandpaper, linseed oil, and the palm of a gun-lover.

Then he went down the steps, and passed out of sight behind the store.

During the silent period of saddling, Mr. Garfield sat perfectly still on the porch railing, his back to the sunset, his cigarette ridging one cheek with a clinging line of smoke, his gaze on the extreme tip of his peg-leg. Only when the slow thud-thud of the ridden horse stopped just behind him did he emerge from immobility and use the peg as a pivot on which to turn and face the rider.

"So long," said the man on the horse.

"So long," said Mr. Garfield. He removed the cigarette and spat out a perfectly genuine flake of tobacco. "Er—goin' anywhere in particular?"

The sunset was behind Arnold; his face was more or less in shadow; but the old man on the porch enjoyed, strangely enough, a perfect view of the young man's eyes. Possibly they were performing the fabulous process of glowing. If so, their glow was far from pleasant; if not, their expression was very peculiar. More than ever, those eyes struck Mr. Garfield as being contemporaneous with his own—his own wrinkle-nested eyes that had taken in seventy-six years of the seamy side of life; but, unlike his own, these eyes seemed to have absorbed what they had seen; and, as if the foreign matter thus lodged had encysted itself, the eyes were as hard as stone.

"Why, yes," said their owner, with a queer mocking smile. "I'm an I. B. C. gunman, you know. I'm just on my way to Hurst County."

CHAPTER III

IT WAS Deputy Sheriff Jake Henson who, in the course of being poetic for the benefit of a lady at Stony Springs ranch, remarked that it seemed a pity such a spring night should have to fall on the undeserving neighbors of Three Pines, as well as on that favored valley; which remark, like most of Mr. Henson's purely social conversation, was noticeable both for its truth, and for the number of times it had been made before. From pre-historic times onward, the cynics of succeeding generations have taken their turns at mocking the Sceneshifter of the human drama; without much effect. To-day, as during Thermopylæ, a desperate battle-field may be visited by a soft breeze bearing the scent of flowers; now, as in the days when Last-Look-About-You Hill was doing such a roaring trade, a man may be hanged with the eight o'clock sun of a summer's morning in his eyes; and, as Mr. Henson so truly said, the dispenser of evenings which, conservatively speaking, are "pleasant for the time of year"—flings them down indiscriminately on peaceful districts and on merry hells.

Perhaps there is an object in it. Who knows?

Over at the Circle R ranch house, in the long low living-room where Joan Bruce sat at a table littered with papers, a jumper to conclusions might have boasted of discovering the reason why this particular evening had been accorded to Hurst County, which for a year or two past had been the merriest hell in the Southwest. He might have guessed, looking into the circle of light from the beaten-copper lamp, that the softness of the air was intended to impart a like quality to the heart of the man who sat opposite the Sage Hen, staring across the table at her with small, bright black eyes. But he would have been quite wrong, as jumpers to conclusions generally are; because, whatever the ingratiating gentleness of Mr. William Rigby's manner, his heart, if he had one, resembled nothing so much as a model in chilled steel, and was about as susceptible to the influence of any softening influences short of an oxyhydrogen blow torch. To put the matter in another way—those who knew Mr.

THE SAGE HEN

Rigby best were accustomed to say his extremely soft pelt concealed meat of an unbelievable toughness; and there were some who added that he would be improved, like other tough meat, by being hung.

Not yet having undergone this improving process, he was one of the numerous attorneys for the International Beef Concern; and this visit to the Circle R was an example of his diligence in his office.

"I assure you, miss," he was saying, with a confirmatory wring of his moist hands, "that so far from coming here to bluster and threaten, as you seem to think, I rode the whole distance from Hurst Seat in fear and trembling, and that when I think of returning thither, or thence, whichever it is, after nightfall, I can hardly contain myself."

The Sage Hen laughed bitterly.

"I should think you'd feel quite secure," she said. "You've got every power in the county behind you, from the sheriff to—"

"If you'll excuse my saying so," Mr. Rigby suggested nervously, "the sheriff's in his office, while several of your—er—rather violent ranch hands are not far away. Some of them looked at me when I arrived in a way which excited my most serious apprehensions. I must repeat, miss, that I am here only to try to adjust peaceably the difference between yourself and my employers; and I assure you, I'm only led to undertake the commission by the thought that I have to—er, forage, as you call it in the West—for my wife and children."

The girl across the table did not tell him that rattlesnakes have the same excuse. Instead, she bent over until her gray eyes commanded a full view of Mr. Rigby's ocular shoe-buttons, and said:

"Your employers want to steal this land, which was granted to my family for its services to the government; they have killed my father and my brother and a dozen other men, trying to do it; they have almost ruined me, and spoiled the ranch itself for the next ten years. What peaceable adjustment is there for that situation?"

"Well, as I suggested—" Mr. Rigby began.

The girl rose, and with a quick motion, snatched away the lamp which, in his innocent way, the lawyer was endeavoring to use as a slight screen, or breastwork against the wrath to come. As she stood there—a leather-skirted Liberty with blazing eyes and the light full on her auburn head—she

THE SAGE HEN

looked vastly handsome. If pity is akin to love, admiration is even more closely related to terror. Mr. Rigby trembled and admired—though he could have wished that the girl's face didn't look quite so drawn and tired.

"You suggested," she flared at him, "that I sell—give this land to your International Thief Concern, and get out with a whole skin. Yes, you did—I understood your 'regrettable eventualities.' You meant that this place is all that prevents you from owning the whole county, and that if I won't give it up by what you call fair means, I must be made to do it by foul."

"My dear young lady—"

The Sage Hen set down the lamp, and leaned across the table with a disarming sweetness.

"If that's not the state of the case, then, my dear young gentleman," she asked, closing her teeth on the last word, "will you kindly tell me what it is?"

Rigby cleared his throat.

"Well," he said nervously, "you know, of course, it's no pleasure—I mean, the International doesn't simply want your ranch to complete its collection, or anything like that— Ha, ha—My employers are not collecting counties as a boy—he-he!—does stamps.

THE SAGE HEN

We have a very good reason for wanting the Circle R. It lies, as I told you, between two of our largest properties, and, my dear lady, you must see perfectly clearly that its independent status puts us to all the trouble, expense, delay and loss of having two round-ups, instead of one. We want the Circle R for the simple business reason that it is val—er—"

"Go on," said Joan Bruce encouragingly, " 'valuable' was the word. Don't trouble to get another one."

"Well—"

"Well, in that case," said the Sage Hen, "if the Circle R is valuable, why don't your valuable employers buy it at its value?"

The lawyer coughed.

"That opens up—I may say—another question," he said, scratching an invisible spot off the table with his finger-nail. "You made another accusation—that I, in my capacity of ambassador, had threatened you with death. I can only remark that if made before witnesses this would be a serious charge, and that—in short—it is untrue. I have carefully refrained from alarming you; and I think if you will search your memory, you will find I have said nothing more threatening than that—er—

THE SAGE HEN

since spring was coming, and since we were being forced to add a large number of additional men to our forces in this county, your position, with the comparatively few men still with you, and the hostility—"

"Those were the exact words," smiled Joan. "Somebody must have written it out for you. But what you mean is that since you've argued all winter without getting anywhere, you're going to bring up fresh troops for the spring campaign, and wipe the floor with me."

Mr. Rigby was horrified. He had, as aforesaid, daughters of his own.

"Wipe the floor—?"

The Sage Hen laughed and drew a slim brown hand across her eyes.

"Oh—wipe the floor—the prairie—put it how you like," she said wearily. "You must excuse my coarseness, Mr. Rigby. You people have left me nobody to talk to but my cowboys—and I suppose I shan't have them long; you hounded one of my best men over into Mexico last week. Probably by the next time you come with a peaceful suggestion, I shall have forgotten how to talk entirely."

"I trust that by that time," said Mr. Rigby, rather loosely, "you will have seen reason, and be recovering your faculties in an eastern environment more fitted—"

The brown hand which had covered the girl's eyes suddenly thudded down on the table and really made him jump.

"Well, I shan't," said the Sage Hen. "I shall be right here—losing my faculties if necessary. The International Beef Concern may be able to buy or bully every other obstacle out of its way, but it can't buy or bully us Bruces. My father died fighting, my brother died fighting; and when—and if— you've captured every square inch of the Circle R but one room in this house, I'll be in that room with a Winchester; and I'll keep on shooting till I'm dead."

For the first time during the negotiations, Mr. Rigby's eyes met the girl's squarely, and without their usual look of boiled opacity. Long habit had made it painful for the gentleman to bare, as it were, his retina in this way; but he was a dutiful servant, and one can not examine anything closely through a mask. It was his duty, at this moment, to

THE SAGE HEN

bring his keenest powers of observation to bear on Miss Joan Bruce, and to decide whether she meant what she said literally or hysterically. He decided that she meant it literally; with a foot-note to the effect that in addition to being a persistent shooter, she was probably a quite efficient shot.

The hypothetical steel of which Mr. Rigby's heart was composed, may be said to have played another large part in the construction of his brain. To liken an intellect to a steel trap is common. Mr. Rigby's mental equipment bore a much stronger resemblance to the time-lock mechanism of a bank-vault door. A touch on the trigger made so many things happen simultaneously; so many tumblers to fall so exactly into place; so many bolts to click into their appointed stations; and, finally, so ponderous a machine to function. For, in speech with Joan Bruce he had quite seriously underestimated himself. He was more than a mere ambassador for his employers; he was, in spite of his shrinking exterior, that terrific combination, a diplomat-general; a military viceroy; the frail controller of the vast power which controlled all—but this strip—of Hurst County; and —with regard to that strip—the commander of the sullen army which at present lounged over its vices in Hurst Seat, and a dozen encircling bunk-houses.

He did not look the part, as he lifted himself carefully out of his chair, smiling vaguely and deprecatingly as he did so. Perhaps he had not been in power long enough for his position to register its impress on his physique; he had only come from Chicago to take command on the field, a month before.

In fact, he still seemed to be the victim of a pitiable cowardice. As he fumbled for his hat, it was quite obvious that his hands were shaking.

"You know," he said, turning toward Joan Bruce a face of perfect terror, "after what you have said, I'm almost afraid—I mean, news travels so fast in these districts, and it's almost impossible to prevent eavesdropping. And your ranchmen—"

"My ranchmen," said the Sage Hen slowly, "have instructions to offer no violence to any one who has not offered them violence first, or attempted to invade this land under arms. They obey me—what there are left of them."

"You remind me," quavered Mr. Rigby, "of something I intended to say in reply to a remark of

THE SAGE HEN

yours, and forgot. Your ranchmen may be all you say; but you must remember, my dear lady, that your cousin—"

"My cousin?"

"Mr. Grant," quavered the lawyer, licking his lips. "Mr. Grant is not your cousin? Oh! I am glad to hear it, because, miss, he is acting, with or without your consent, in a manner which will certainly get him into serious trouble eventually, and which is one of the reasons why the International Beef Concern is beginning to fear that it may be compelled to meet force with force in your case. I don't mean any offense—I know, of course, that you contend that the violence heretofore has been entirely on our side— Dear me, where was I? I am really in such a nervous condition—"

"I guess you mean you'd like me to give you a safe-conduct off the Circle R?" asked Joan Bruce—and rang a bell.

Instantaneously, the door of the living-room was flung violently open, and a vast cowboy named Sloan not only entered, but, before the tingle of the bell had died, was posted threateningly two feet from the shrinking lawyer, hands on gun butts.

"Did you ring, ma'am?" asked this apparition, his eyes on Rigby's face, his voice a vibrating bass growl.

"Sloan!" snapped the Sage Hen.

Mr. Sloan detached his gaze and permitted himself to relax slightly.

"Ma'am?"

"Take this gentleman," said Joan Bruce, "and—"

"My dear lady—my dear lady!" babbled the viceroy, "I meant a personal safe-conduct—yourself in person. If you would ride with me—"

"Why, you—" began the huge cowboy.

"Sloan!"

There was a much longer interval; then:

"Ma'am?"

"Saddle my horse; bring it and Mr. Rigby's in front *muy pronto*."

For people he likes, the free-born and free-grown-up cowpuncher will condescend to equal, in the capacities of cook, groom, and even butler, the best of English servants—except in one respect; impassivity.

"Do you mean to tell me," roared Sloan, "that you're goin' ridin', miss, with this guy who's just—"

THE SAGE HEN

"I mean to tell you nothing more than you seem to have heard at the door," said the Sage Hen icily; "except what I have told you already—to get the horses."

The big man's hands dangled helplessly.

"Well, will you let me, an' Teddy, an'—"

"No."

Mr. Sloan visibly thought—slowly, as befitted a bulk made more for power than for quick turning. Then he as visibly brightened up.

"All right," he said; and with a murderous look which shattered Mr. Rigby still more, turned and clumped bow-leggedly out.

Five minutes later, the girl and her deadly enemy were riding side by side across the plain which stretched between the Circle R ranch house and the town of Hurst Seat.

CHAPTER IV

IT WAS a brilliantly moonlit night; though the moon had not the poetic bare heavens in which to look about herself. The winds of March, exiled to the upper levels, had been trying out their youthful strength upon some soft, good-natured cloud-masses, which now, in agonized shreds, were flying across the blue ceiling of the night, pursued by their too-rough playmates. Rather an alarming night, Mr. Rigby thought, shivering slightly in his saddle. The clouds cast shadows that looked—well, looked like—it was really very difficult to say just what those shadows did look like; but the alarming thing about them was the speed with which they traveled. They fell upon the gray prairie a mile away, and in the instant, had sped soundlessly up to one—and past. Eerie. And then again, an occasional slant of wind from above would perform most nerve-shattering tricks with a pine-tree or a mesquite bush, or a clump of sage—making it bow, or rattle, or

THE SAGE HEN

rustle for an instant, without disturbing the surrounding vegetation, or sending any explanatory gust of breeze into an observer's face.

Mr. Rigby permitted himself a full-sized shudder and pulled his gray silk scarf a little more closely about his throat. He did not feel chilly; but to admit that one has shivered on a warm night, is to impugn one's conscience, and Mr. Rigby's conscience was one of his greatest assets. It was only the promptings of this impalpable organ, as he had frequently told persons likely to be interested, which enabled him to carry out his duty to his employers in face of the frequent unpleasantness which arose.

"Is that a path?" he asked, pointing to a ribbon of moonlit dust which drove away on the right, toward the hills.

The girl at his side smiled.

"It's what we call a trail," she said, looking at it wistfully. "It's the trail to Three Pines. Do you know, Mr. Lawyer, you rather encourage me. You don't know the first thing about this section, do you —and I hear most of your thugs are new since last year."

"We find it advisable," said Mr. Rigby, "to

transfer our employees about from time to time—to widen their experience. In view of the—lamentable events—of last year, we thought it best to exchange staffs between Hurst County and—certain other properties of ours."

The Sage Hen laughed.

"What's the matter, miss?"

"I was just thinking that if all these new men are off your properties, you must own several jails. You even shipped your last year's sheriff away, didn't you?"

"Another—sheriff—has recently been elected. I—I believe Mr. Martin's health required him to —travel."

Joan laughed again.

"You'll excuse me," she said, "but you really are awfully funny. Do you know what was wrong with his health? Why, after Martin had said that my brother's murder was my brother's own fault, old Bill Garfield, from Three Pines—the sheriff, you know—came over. He didn't get the murderer; but he went and saw Martin. Uncle Bill used to be a Ranger, and he's kind of touchy about the way peace-officers behave themselves. He told your late sheriff that the next trick he pulled of the kind, he'd come over, in his seventy-oddth year, and cut Mr. Martin's ears off, and run the Hurst County sheriffship himself!"

"That would be in the highest degree illegal!" gasped Rigby. Then he gasped again. "What's that?"

The girl turned her head in the direction of his pointed finger. "It's a man," she said slowly, "riding along the trail from Three Pines. But it isn't old Bill Garfield. It's too tall."

There was a pause.

"My property ends at that pine thicket," said the Sage Hen, a minute later, "and that's where I leave you. Hurst Seat's four miles straight ahead. You can see the glow in the sky—and hear the clink of the glasses, I should imagine."

"I trust I haven't offended you?" asked the lawyer, his eyes fixed ahead with a strange intensity, on the pine thicket which showed black against the gray of the prairie.

"To hear you talking about illegality was rather sickening," said Joan Bruce levelly; "but never mind that. What are you so nervous about?"

THE SAGE HEN

They were almost in the shadow of the thicket now; and Rigby, his eyes more like black shoebuttons than ever, had suddenly craned his neck to stare backward over his shoulder at the plain across which they had ridden.

"If it's the Three Pines trail man you're afraid of," said Joan pityingly, "you needn't be. He's taking no notice of you—or us. We're not *all* gunmen around here, sir. We go about our business—"

The lawyer stared ahead again.

"I was not apprehensive that the man might attack me," he said steadily, yet in a voice which trembled slightly, "I feared rather that he might be tempted to interfere in a matter which is really for your own good. I—"

The Sage Hen's hand wrenched viciously back on her pony's bridle.

"What do you mean?" she cried, alarmed, her free hand seeking the automatic pistol in its holster at her side.

With quite unexpected promptness, and with the steely grip of a man who fears inefficiency may cost him a perforated skull, Mr. Rigby's moist bony hand shot forward and clutched her gun wrist.

THE SAGE HEN

"Come on!" shrieked the lawyer's voice urgently.

And at the word of command, a dozen mounted men spurred out of the black pool of shadow which surrounded the pine copse, and formed a close-ringed escort about the pair. One of them, who seemed to carry the shadow with him, even when the moon shone full on his face—a gigantic negro, wearing a fantastic Mexican hat decorated with silver dollars—leaned forward to take the pistol from Joan's hand.

"Gimme!" he snarled, as her obstinate fingers clutched the butt. His black fist hammered cruelly on the back of the girl's hand. "Gimme! Ah, you white hell-cat—"

With a desperate effort, Joan had swung her other hand over, worked the slide of the automatic pistol, and then, with the last spasmodic contraction of her forefinger before the whole of her right hand was paralyzed, fired one shot, which reechoed sharply from the sounding-board formed by the trees, backward across the plain. The next instant, the gun was wrenched from her hand, and her wrist twisted until, against her will, she shrieked with agony.

"I teach you try to shoot me!" snarled the negro.

"We'd better drag our freight," called one of the white men sharply. "That guy that was ridin' on the trail there's heard that shot an' stopped. Say, he's comin'. We better shake it out o' this!"

The negro dropped Joan's wrist, and turned to stare from under the brim of his hat, at the advancing horseman.

"He comin' out of a li'l bank of mist," said the mellow voice with a strange brooding note, "he goin' into a big bank of mist soon."

"James!" snapped Rigby, "we must go!"

The black man turned toward the lawyer.

"I runs de killin' end," he said, still in that brooding tone. "Boss, I de white man's butcher. Dis guy see too much. We don't want him trailin', an' informin', an' sich. We wait for him here, an' I have his heart's blood."

He drew a long knife; and, as he felt its edge, his eyes turned again to the advancing rider, his white companions, his white boss, his white prisoner paralyzed with horror behind him, broke into a strange, wild chant on three notes; a bloodcurdling drone in the queer hushed voice of a sleep-walker:

"O-o-o-oeee, o-o-o-o-i,
De snake—crawl—through—de—dead man's—eye
O-o-o-o-i!

"He comin' to the slaughter—come on, white man —feel de nigger's knife—no, nigger come to you."

His voice rose suddenly to a terrifying bellow.

"Here's for de whip an' the lash, de cord an' de brandin'-iron. O-o-o-o-o-e-e-e-e!"

The next instant, his pony, gored on flank and neck by the spurs and the point of the knife, had shot forward like a thunderbolt. Two shots were fired; and then, with a thud, the two ponies met shoulder to shoulder. The knife flashed high, poised for an instant, and flashed down.

"Aah!" came a hoarse yell of pain.

"That's James!" muttered one of the men in the escort.

"Then go help him!" snarled Rigby. "Three of you! I've got the girl!"

Half a dozen of the men started forward; but it was not destined that their rôle should be that of attackers. They had progressed perhaps ten yards away from their former station when they saw the two figures locked together, wrestling, on the backs of the close-pressed ponies, give a mighty heave, and separate into the component figures of the tall white man, and the murderous black. Frisco James' right arm hung limply by his side, its wrist dislocated by a similar, but more terrible wrench than he had applied to Joan's slim arm. The white man's right hand was at his throat, forcing the bullet head, still hatted, backward until the tall crown of the sombrero was almost horizontal, and the ebony jaw pointed upward at the moon. And suddenly, a line of darkness—the white man's left arm—sketched itself for an instant between the level of the saddle and the point of the jaw.

With a gurgling choke, Frisco James shot backward, to hang head-downward with one leg, stirrup-held, strained to breaking-point across the horn of his saddle.

And in the same instant, the man who had knocked him out had yelled frightfully and made his horse leap forward to another attack.

Two men he shot dead; a third, with a thrust of the revolver barrel whose filed foresight made it barbed, he poked off his horse to lie writhing, one eye blinded, until the ponies' milling hoofs dashed out his brains. Then, with the strange insanity which will sometimes afflict the coolest of fighters in action, the attacker dropped the hand gun which still contained two cartridges, disregarded the other revolver which hung fully loaded at his belt, and, as the three remaining men of the advance-guard closed in on him, made a desperate attempt to pull a Winchester from its gun bucket.

He realized his error as a pair of steel-like arms wrapped around his shoulders; but then it was too late. He broke that grip with a sudden duck and wrench to one side, and bowled that adversary off his horse with a lucky smash of the elbow under the ear; but other hands were on him—crushing his throat, tearing his gun belt and rifle away, and, as he struggled, he saw a half-dozen other men, revolvers ready, riding forward to the assistance of these. He was done for, all right—but if he was going to die, what was going to happen to the girl? Once, in New Mexico, he had helped stake out three men, naked, on an ant-hill in the blazing sun; and the tale of what those long-picked bones had done to deserve the frightful death, came hammering into his mind with far more force than some unseen person's fists were hammering at his temple. Unconsciousness was dazing his thoughts. Was there a girl in this business, anyhow? Yes—he'd seen her and a man riding past as he came along the trail yonder. But how did he know—his foot came out of the stirrup at last, and dealt a murderous kick that seemed to discourage the beating of his temples—how did he know she was in this mess? Pure guess—and he was going to be killed for it.

Then, as if in a snapshot taken between the shoulders of two men, he saw her. At the same instant, every muscle in his writhing body relaxed and slumped.

"God," he heard a breathless voice say above him.

"He knocked my gun out of my hand," said another, "blow his brains out, Jimmy!"

"Awright."

The hammer of the single action revolver had clicked only once under the thumb of the executioner, when John Arnold returned to life, and sat upright, driving out his fists to right and left with the force he had been gathering as he lolled back limp in his saddle, to the targets he had selected through just-opened lids. Jimmy, his revolver still at half-cock, felt the bone of his nose break and grate; the man who had dropped his gun made a ghastly retching sound as a frightful blow took him in the stomach.

"Up, Jinny!" shouted Arnold then, and heaved violently on his bridle.

There were three men left still—not counting that guy in black by the girl's side—no, he was going. Jinny, rearing almost upright, lashing out blindly with her iron-shod forefeet, disposed of one; his horse fell, stunned; so suddenly that the rider's left leg was ground out of all rigidity.

Now, another rear toward the left—

But to do that, it was necessary to turn away from the attacker on the right, and he—

Jinny reared again; and that instant, John Arnold's own rifle-barrel, wielded by the enemy behind him, swung in a vicious arc and smashed home on its target—the back of the head. Instantly unconscious, yet obeying a residual instinct which made him kick his senseless feet out of the stirrups, the man who had fought twelve threw his arms wide and fell backward.

"Now!" said the man who had stunned him.

"Look out!" yelled his surviving companion.

The warning was given only just in time, according to the ruffians' manners of expressing it; and only a few seconds too early, in the view of the knot of Circle R punchers, headed by Sloan, who now burst into view, their horses trailed by wisps of mist from the fog bank, a hundred yards away.

"I know this guy!" cried the wielder of the Winchester, as his eyes, stupid and incredulous, looked from his victim's face, upturned in the moonlight, to the charging cavalcade.

"Come on, you damn fool!" shouted his companion. "Those are the skirt's punchers!"

These words broke the trance with which the recognition of Arnold seemed to have bound the other thug. Next moment, the two survivors, spurs raking madly, barbed-wire bits jammed cruelly back, had wrenched their ponies around and started at full speed for Hurst Seat; whither Mr. Rigby, his respectable black coat and gray silk muffler flying in the wind of his progress, had preceded them.

"Shall we chase 'em, miss?" demanded Sloan, reining his pony to its haunches, and flinging a vast

THE SAGE HEN

arm around the shoulders of his boss as she swayed in her saddle.

The girl shook her head.

"Look after him," she whispered, pointing to the prostrate figure at which Jinny was now nosing, with heart-broken whickers of inquiry as to whether this were her fault. "Take him back to—ranch-house. He saved me—"

"Been no need of 'm if you hadn't scared us to foller you closer'n a mile," growled Sloan; and then coughed out an oath and tightened his grip. "Hey, miss, I didn't mean—ow, God! She ain't dead, is she?" He twisted in his saddle and yelled to the men who were lifting John Arnold.

"Drop that goof!" blubbered the big brute who was holding the Sage Hen. "She's died on me! She's dead!"

A young man named (locally) Spoofendinkel, who had ceased studying medicine at Munich at the request of the Imperial German Government, came forward and took the girl's wrist.

"Fainted," he said. "Bud if I meed de man vat tvist her wrist like dis, he die on himself all right. See, she gums to herself now. Ve sdart back?"

"Yes. Ain't I got a bad enough cold already?" roared Sloan, in reference to his streaming eyes.

"Und de vounded enemey?" asked Spoofendinkel, casually turning the negro's face away with his foot.

"There's buzzards," said Sloan.

It was, of course, no proper speech for a hero— for even a minor hero; it was, as every educated person knows, a remark which should have been left unsaid pending the appearance of a large, glossy villain with black mustaches, who could snarl it through his polished white teeth. But Mr. Sloan, upon whom the reading of fiction conferred a violent headache, was not educated; unless it is possible to apply that noble term to fifteen years of experience on the frontier, and twenty-four months on the Circle R ranch; which experience had taught him nothing more heroic, gentlemanly, or sportsmanlike than the doctrine that a fight's main object is victory, and that a mere consciousness of fair-play will plug no bullet-holes. Mr. Sloan was in a hard country, fighting men so utterly hard that their souls would have made the celebrated nether millstone seem like butter in comparison; and he held the idea that any softness on his part would be to his disadvantage—and to that of the Circle R. So, both for his own sake and for his employer's, he eschewed the fictional behavior of people who are in the right, until such time as the International Beef Concern should see the great fictional light of Sportsmanship, and issue their prison-trained cohorts orders to behave like chivalrous enemies.

To come back to concrete facts, he who had proved his willingness to bankrupt himself for a pal, and to risk his life daily for the Sage Hen, not only advised leaving the fallen foe to his own devices, or those of nature's scavengers, but did it.

CHAPTER V

WHEN they were nearly at the Circle R, Joan cried suddenly that some of the men they had left on the moonlit prairie might be only wounded, and that they must go back.

"We ain't got any hawses, we ain't got any medicines, we don't want a bunch of thugs living right among us," said Mr. Sloan, "and we ain't goin' back. Drag ahead, Spoofendinkel. I'm boss here."

The Sage Hen's temper flared.

"You're boss?" she cried, wrenching herself out of the arms which supported her in her saddle.

"While you're sick," said Mr. Sloan equably, and caught her as she swayed again. "Whatchew lookin' back at, Corliss?"

The ranch-house windows were now in sight and Corliss, who was afflicted with long sight so acute as to make him the equal of a five-dollar telescope, had been exercising his talent.

"Just wanted to say," he remarked hoarsely, "that there's a guy in the livin'-room, pacin' up an' down like a tiger with the stomachache."

"Probably Mr. International Beef," said Sloan. "I'd like to meet that guy. I'd give him something to be concerned about. Get that, Spoofendinkel? International Beef *Concern,* see?"

There was a belated groan, which was accepted as a compliment, and then Corliss spoke again.

"Why," he said, when they were a hundred yards from the windows, "it's young Mr. Grant!"

"Grant!" cried Joan, wrenching herself upright.

"Don't excite yourself, miss," said Sloan.

"You'll throw him off my land as soon as we reach the house, Sloan!" the girl cried.

There was a regretful silence. The punchers of the Circle R liked this chap who wanted to marry their boss. They hoped he wouldn't get hanged on his guerrilla expeditions, and they wished they could be along to see that he wasn't. But their duty was to their salt, and it was forbidden.

"Sloan, you hear me? Corliss—"

"All right, ma'am," said the observatory sadly. "After what's happened to-night, I should think—

THE SAGE HEN

'And he's got a black eye already. An' a split lip."

"He must leave—at once," said the Sage Hen.

But he did not. When the cavalcade had dismounted, Joan found herself, strangely, too weary and weak to issue new orders; and her men, standing with the limp body of John Arnold in their midst, and looking at the battered man who stood facing them across the lamplit table, did not feel any great inclination to carry out those she had already given. There was a look in young Grant's face—

"Good evening, boys," he said, smiling slightly, and changing the end of his sentence as Joan, her face averted from him, sank down in a saddlebag chair.

His eyes took in the burden carried between Corliss and another man, by the head and heels. Stepping from behind the table, and carrying the lamp with him, he approached the group.

"Got some one?" he asked.

Mr. Sloan's mind, as has been hinted, moved slowly. This new development caught him in the midst of formulating an inquiry, and the process of formulation was too majestic to be stopped.

"Who banged you up like that, Dave?" he therefore asked brightly, just as Grant brought the circle of light to bear on the unconscious face of Arnold.

A gasp of surprise preceded his answer.

"Why," cried Grant, "this chap did!"

Mr. Sloan's jaw dropped.

"This chap? Why, whatever for? Whatchew fightin' him for, Dave? He's just after rescuin' Miss Joan here from a bunch of I. B. C. men that wanted to kidnap her."

"Rescued her—from a bunch of—I. B. C. men?" asked David Grant slowly.

He put the lamp back on the table.

"Sloan," he said, "you remember I told you I'd beaten the tar out of a Beef man who'd just come in from Mexico, and that I was going to beat the tar out of another that was expected—another gunman?"

"Yeah."

"Well, this is the second man."

There was an appalled silence.

"Did he—did he—admit it?" asked Corliss in a hoarse whisper.

"Yes!"

THE SAGE HEN

It was fortunate that Mr. Corliss' end of the unconscious man was the feet; because whichever end he had held, he would have dropped it, as he now did. Packy Deans, who held the big man's head, was of a less sudden disposition. When he felt that his convictions, too, would permit him no further intercourse with Mr. Arnold, he resigned his burden gently to the ingrain carpet.

It was distinctly unjust, then, that Joan, entering the discussion with all the miniature ferocity of the bird whose name she bore, should choose Packy's bronzed cheek to slap with all the force of her hard little hand.

"Pick him up again, you cowards," she cried. "Lay him on that sofa. Is this dude master here, or am I? I'll give the orders—and I'll bring the news. This swaggering swashbuckler's the cause of half the violence around here. The man who obeys him can go with him—out of this house. Out, you, Grant!"

Grant did not move.

"Sloan!"

The big man turned from his task of laying Arnold on the designated couch.

"Ma'am?"

"Throw him out!"

There was a silence.

"Well, Sloan?" asked David Grant.

"She's my boss," said the slow puncher, "not you. I sure wish you two could get together an' make an alliance of it, instead of scrappin' between yourselves thisaway, when you know you both—"

"Sloan, are you—"

"Yes, ma'am. She's my boss, Dave, an' if she says so—out you go."

The lamplit tableau remained immobile for perhaps five seconds; and then, with a sudden start, and a sudden craning of bronzed necks, and the shuffling of many pairs of twenty-dollar boots, it broke up like the banks of cigarette smoke above its head.

"Out who goes?" came a polite, inquiring voice from the couch.

John Arnold had recovered consciousness.

He arose, and turned the blankly puzzled face typical of concussion cases, to right and left of him.

"I don't quite—" he began; then saw Joan. His eyes flickered with awakening memory, glanced past her, as if in search of confirmation, and came to rest on Dave Grant, standing isolated by the table.

"Why, hello, buddy!" Arnold paused, put a hand to his aching head, and then chuckled. "Don't tell me it's you that's getting thrown out?"

"Yes, it is!" Grant took a sudden step forward. "What have you got to say about it?"

Arnold chuckled again, reflectively, as if words were filtering into his consciousness very slowly.

"It seems to be your busy day," he remarked; and then, swaying suddenly to one side, grasped at the proverbial straw to keep himself from falling, and caught Sloan's shoulder.

"Say," growled the big puncher, twisting his head around until he faced the wounded man, "are you workin' for the I. B. C.?"

Weakly, his eyes half closed as he listened to a complicated ringing of bells and firing of salutes inside his head, Arnold nodded.

"Then you can get to hell off me," said Sloan; and with a violent heave of the shoulders, withdrew his support. Arnold staggered, stumbled over his own feet, and crumpled down, sitting, by the side of the couch. At the jar of his fall, which rocked his splitting head on his shoulders, he groaned briefly, tried to rise, but sank back, breathing heavily, his face pale, his eyes closed.

"I'll kill you for that, when I'm better," he whispered.

"For two pins," roared Sloan, "I'd put a bullet through you right now, where you lie, you skunk!"

The eyes of the fallen man opened, and he made a second attempt to rise. It was as he reached his feet, and as Sloan's hand dropped willingly to a gun butt, that the mistress of Circle R intervened. She tore herself from the restraining grasp of Corliss, and stood between the two men.

"Sloan—" she began furiously.

Without unfixing his gaze from that of his adversary, John Arnold pushed her gently aside.

"Excuse me, miss," he said. And then to Sloan: "You don't seem to talk my language, friend. Here I've got hurt pulling a lady out—"

He stopped suddenly.

"Why—"

It was a gasp of enlightenment, and as he looked around, he saw the grim faces of the men around

THE SAGE HEN

him cracking into grins of mockery as the jest dawned upon them, too.

"He didn't know it!" shouted Sloan, the last to divine the meaning of the pause. "He didn't know it! He's sent here to fight the Sage Hen, an' the first thing he does is to kill half a dozen of his friends an' rescue her from 'em! He didn't know it! Oh, haw-haw-haw!"

"What Ol' Boss Beef will say to *him!*" cried a voice; and there was another roar. There is no means, in fact, of knowing how long the Circle R men would have continued to honor with their bellows the first joke in two years which had not been on themselves; for they had not really started, when the wet blanket was applied. They paused for an instant to gather breath for fresh elaborations of the subject, and for cachinnations to match; and into that pause there cut the icy voice of their boss, saying clearly:

"Get out!"

She stood by the side of her tattered rescuer, a slim tense figure with blazing eyes.

"Get out!" she repeated, "you lot of cowards, you laughing coyotes; get out of this room—and off the

THE SAGE HEN

ranch, if you feel like it. No sick men are going to be baited here."

Sloan protested.

"Well, ma'am—"

She gave him her undivided attention.

"You," she said through her teeth, "have been acting foreman since Dryden ran away to Mexico. You seem to think that gives you the right to disobey me. Well, you're not foreman any more. Now get out—get right out. I don't want you around the Circle R at all."

Mr. Sloan gave this his best thought.

"I'll leave the room, if you like, miss," he said. "But I ain't goin' off this land, except feet first. Promised your dad."

"Get out!" said the girl again.

"An' leave you with—this thug?"

"He rescued me," said the Sage Hen bitterly, "when you would have been just a little too late."

This was felt to be cruelly unjust, but at the same time, a reply on the spur of the moment was beyond the big man's intellectual powers. Nor did the vicious twisting of his hat produce inspiration of the necessary quality. He therefore perspired profusely and rolling his eyes agonizedly in the direction of Dave Grant, who stood motionless in his old position by the table, retreated toward the door, his former command backing awkwardly out before him. Out in the passage, endeavoring to decide whether to retire to the bunk-house in dudgeon, or to hang around in case his services should be needed after all, he heard four remarks by the trio remaining in the room.

John Arnold's voice, weak, wondering, and rather amused, was saying:

"Of course—of course! Why didn't I know—"

"The door's still open," said Joan Bruce coldly. "I shall be obliged if you'll close it after you, Mr. Grant."

"I'm not going out," replied David, "until this fellow goes with me." There was a silence of deadlock, broken by Arnold's words, as he walked unsteadily over toward the listening punchers:

"I'd let him stay, miss. He—"

And then the door slammed shut.

"He seems," continued John Arnold, "to have kind of an interest in you, miss. And I guess you need all the friends you can get."

THE SAGE HEN

"Including yourself, I suppose?" Dave Grant threw at him.

The injured man seated himself rather suddenly on the couch.

"Excuse me, miss. Well, yes,—including myself."

"When you came to this county to fight for the I. B. C.!"—

Arnold was studying the backs of his hands.

"Well, as regards that," he said slowly, "perhaps I ought to explain to you, buddy; especially after that beating I gave you this afternoon. I wish you'd take a seat, Miss Joan—and you too. I feel kind of uncomfortable sitting down when you're standing, and I don't feel able to stand, much, myself."

Pointedly, Grant took no notice of the invitation. As pointedly, with an angry look at him, Joan Bruce accepted it.

"I came here to—work for the Beef Concern," Arnold went on, "because that's the way I earn my living. I wasn't lending my gun to any holy cause." He stopped, and frowned as if over some problem. When he spoke again, his young-old eyes, under brows still corrugated with thought, were fixed on the face of Joan Bruce. "I'm—I guess you'd call it—a soldier of fortune. Well, I—seem to have queered myself with my employers, all right—don't I?"

He smiled. With a rather obvious effort, the Sage Hen responded in kind.

"Well, then," said David Grant, "you mean that you'll turn around now, and get back into Mexico, or wherever you came from?"

Arnold, still frowning, returned to the examination of the backs of his hands.

"No," he said slowly, "I wasn't thinking of doing that."

"What are you going to do?"

"Oh—stick around."

"At Circle R, I suppose?"

"If the lady'll let me."

Grant drew a long breath through his teeth.

"You treacherous thug, you!"

The next instant, Arnold was on his feet, facing Dave as closely as they had faced each other before the fight of that afternoon.

"Look here, young man," said a deep voice vi-

THE SAGE HEN

brant with menace, "you're young, and you're in love, and you're a fool, and I make allowances for you; but there are some things I'll take off no man. Mark me! I'm a bad man, and I don't care who knows it; I know it myself; but I'll be bad the way I feel like, without any comments. You've fought me, and you're still on your two feet. Thank God for that, and don't presume on it; because as sure as you say another word like the last, I'll cripple you for the rest of your life."

The Sage Hen's voice, strangely hoarse and trembling, cut in.

"Oh, don't! David—David—please go!"

"No," said Grant, without moving. His eyes still held those of the battered man whose stare blazed death. "You can go as far as you like, stranger; and what I have to say, I'll say. You're ready to dodge from one side of this fight to the other because it suits you; and if you shoot me right now, I'll warn Miss Bruce that a man who'll do that, will dodge back again if it suits him."

Suddenly, he stepped aside.

"Joan," he cried, "don't treat me like this! Can't you see what I'm doing? I'm sick with dread for you. You claim I'm making your job on the ranch harder by—by what I'm doing; yet you force me to it by not letting me help you fight the I. B. C. as I want to. I can't leave you in danger alone! You know why— And if you'd meant what you said—"

"I don't think that's a matter to discuss before—this gentleman," said the Sage Hen with an effort.

Grant stopped.

"No," he said slowly. "No. But this is. Before this ranch business came up—before your father and brother were killed—you—were going to give me the right—to look after you. Well—that's all right . . . you don't seem to think, now, that I'm capable of doing it."

"You don't understand the situation here!" the girl cried.

"I understand this," cried Grant, "you want to take this man on the ranch—this I. B. C. man who's turned away from his wickedness. And I remember something. It's no time to mince words. Who murdered your brother? A train-robber he'd picked up fresh out of jail, and given a job on the Circle R to reform him. There was a sinner turned away from his wickedness—until the I. B. C. cov-

THE SAGE HEN

eted this ranch and offered him more money to turn back again. Now you're going to do the same thing."

The girl, white-faced, her hand over her heart, had risen from her chair. Grant, as pale as she, was trembling in every limb. Down John Arnold's chin, from the spot in his lip where his white teeth were cutting into the red, trickled a drop of blood.

"I guess you went a little too far that time, David," he said, so unsteadily that the words seemed to climb upon one another.

"Remember that!" whispered David Grant.

"I do remember it," said the Sage Hen almost inaudibly.

"Then—what are you going to do?"

"I'm going to manage my own affairs," said Joan Bruce slowly, "and stand or fall by my own judgment. This is my fight, Dave Grant, and I'll fight it my own way. I've begged you to leave me alone; you've persisted in interfering; and—every time you have done so, it has made matters worse for me. Yes, it has! You've given the I. B. C. all the excuse they want for violence—you've presented them with evidence that they can twist to show that

THE SAGE HEN

all the trouble this year will be my fault. You've made my punchers here on the ranch dissatisfied with me. It was through going on the war-path with you that Dryden had to get over the border—the best man I had. You saw to-night that Sloan will not obey me. Now you're ordering me to tell a man who's saved my life, that he's a Judas, and to turn down his offer of help. You need a lesson. I'll give it to you." She turned toward Arnold. "I don't know your name—"

Gravely, he told it to her.

"Well, Mr. Arnold, I thank you for what you did to-night. I'm sorry for what Mr. Grant has seen fit to say. But to show that I don't—agree with him—will you become foreman of the Circle R? I—don't think I need—explain the difficulties of the job."

"Joan!" David cried out in agonized protest.

"Gives me pleasure," said the wounded man, his eyes on the face of David Grant, "to accept. Thank you, Miss Joan."

Of just what happened in the smoky, lamplit room after that, there is no accurate record. Two of the actors on the scene were too exhausted by emotion to remember; the third was too badly hurt, and too confused by the revolutionary events of the evening, to recall anything but a hysterical promise, by David Grant, to kill him on sight. The only authorities whose record might have been dispassionate—Sloan, and his fellows, in the passage—had adjourned at the moment of the acceptance of the foremanship, to hold an indignation meeting which, under the rafters of the bunk-house, rumbled like distant thunder; though Corliss, taking his phenomenal eyesight outside at the sound of Grant's wild mounting of his horse, came back with a confused story about the I. B. C. man's standing on the porch, holding himself upright by a pillar, and saying, in a low tone:

"Trust me, boy! Both about the ranch—and about—the other matter."

But if the end of the evening at the Circle R is rather vague as to details, elsewhere it was closing with events only too definitely relevant.

Out on the prairie, near a pine copse, whose shadow, with the rising of the moon, had moved until a huddle of bodies and a bunch of grazing horses were fully illumined by the pale blue light of the moon, a vast negro was crawling out, on all fours, from under a dead white man. He found his horse, and mounted; then, shaking his fist, and baring his blood-flecked teeth toward the Circle R ranch house, turned and galloped furiously in the direction of Hurst Seat. Back through the soft night mist, to the little battle-field, there floated the sound of a chant from the Congo, shrieked in a high eerie key.

—"the snake crawl through the dead man's eye
  O-o-o-o-i!"

At the same hour, having arrived at Three Pines on a foam-bespattered pony, and invoked the aid of an extremely disapproving and sleepy Mr. Garfield as a brother officer of the law, the sheriff of Hurst County was thumbing over a large collection of posters, varied in text and illustration, but all alike in that their head-lines, in big black type, consisted of the one word:

WANTED

CHAPTER VI

BY AND LARGE, it had been a wild night; and it might easily—nay, certainly would—have continued into a still wilder early morning, had the new foreman, following the close of his conference with his new boss, done the logical thing, and taken his weariness and wounds to bed in the bunk-house.

This, however, he did not do. Instead, with the grave statement that he believed he had dropped something back there where the fight was, he borrowed Joan Bruce's horse—which, standing neglected and shivering by the porch railing, testified mutely to the punchers' state of mind—and, mounting, rode thoughtfully away from the Circle R through a cold dawn dampened by lifting mists. He not only rode thoughtfully but—a quite different thing—he was thinking; and apparently his cogitations were not of the most soothing. As he passed the debouchement of the Three Pines trail, for instance, he laughed mockingly at himself and shook his head; a few minutes later, picking up from the wet grass of the battle-field his own pet Winchester, with which his own pet cerebellum had been dealt such a frightful blow, he shook his head again, and muttered, "Damn fool!"—also to his own address. The rifle's muzzle was plugged with dirt; the foresight was bent enough to give twenty inches windage at a hundred yards; and on the velvety surface of the butt a pony had left the mark of a large splay hoof.

With an effort, Arnold detached his eyes from this outrage; and working the breech mechanism with a careful absent-mindedness designed to cushion the shock if it jammed, gave a shrill whistle, twice repeated. A moment later, there was a soft whicker from behind the pine copse, and Jinny came into view.

"Come here, fool," said her master, smiling.

She came rather doubtfully, whinnying at every four steps; and, when she reached his side, stretched out her neck and laid her head on his shoulder with the unrelieved weight which marks equine affection.

"Very nice," said John Arnold, "but why didn't you trail along after me, eh? Get off, you old slut.

Lean on me any more, and you'd knock me down. Blankets!"

Briskly, the mare withdrew her head and turned her right side. Detaching his bedding-roll from behind the saddle, the man rested his hand momentarily on her shoulder, then drew it backward along the wiry coat, and crisped fingers and thumb together. Jinny was not shivering, nor was she damp with sweat—she was a Mexican breed, with a skin designed for higher temperatures than had prevailed during her gallop earlier in the night. Nevertheless, having detached two blankets, Arnold flung one of them over her back, and, in the absence of straps on its edges, tucked its four down-hanging corners under the *chincha*. He made a vague motion or two toward unsaddling; but he was too tired; the pony, now nuzzling his knee, seemed to understand.

"Dance, old lady," he commanded, pointing to a spot ten yards removed from the huddle of bodies, and the group of ponies standing at gaze, near by. And while Jinny, taking station at the indicated point, gravely thudded the earth to scare out possible rattlers and tarantulas from their holes, her master walked rather unsteadily over to the grim tableau. It seemed to have lost a certain quality of awesomeness with the waxing of the light. Death looks very mean in the dawn—especially if the observer's mouth is dry, his eyes smarting, and his head aching violently from injury and lack of sleep.

It was extremely annoying, moreover, that as Arnold bent to replace his lost revolver with a gun from the belt of a fallen enemy, that the man should move one arm feebly, and groan; though, after a muttered remark expressing his emotions at finding sleep delayed again, the foreman of the Circle R dealt with the annoyance rapidly and effectively. There were three men who seemed to be only wounded. With difficulty, he picked them up, one after another, bound them across the saddles of three of the grazing ponies, securing their pendent heads and feet together with riatas from the saddles; and then, with a sharp cut of the quirt on each flank, and a *"Vaya con Dios!"* at which he laughed weakly, started the animals off for their homes. It was an even chance that they would go somewhere else, or, in spite of their burdens, go nowhere in particular at all, but he could do no more; and in fact, cursed himself for a soft-hearted fool, for exhausting his last strength doing so much. Dragging his blanket over his shoulder, he could scarcely stagger to the pounded spot upon which Jinny awaited him; and, having reached it, he fell down overtaken by sleep from which he awoke, shivering, an hour later, to roll himself cocoon-fashion, in his bedding.

After that, he lay as one dead until the sun, swinging high, shone redly through his eyelids, at half past nine.

Then, sitting bolt upright, a hand, from force of habit, closing on the gun butt which had lain convenient during unconsciousness, he said "Ooooooh!" yawned, stretched, and climbed to his feet. He had slept eight hours, and felt like a giant refreshed with wine—the morning after the refreshment, for he still had a headache.

On the other side of the pine copse, the boundary of the Circle R was marked by a gulley, which, dry in summer, was at present the bed of a sizable spring freshet from the hills. Extracting a small coffee pot from the war bag on Jinny's withers, Arnold filled it with ice-cold water, set it down on the bank of the stream; and then, leisurely undressing, flopped bodily into the torrent. The temperature was very little above freezing; but the dip seemed to do him good. He emerged, blowing like a whale, pinched water out of his nose with a thumb and finger, shook it out of his ears with a vigor that made his head throb, dried himself sketchily with his shirt, which he then spread on a clump of chaparral, and, pulling on the rest of his clothes, except his boots, seized his coffee pot and proceeded to build a fire. While the pot boiled, he put on his boots; then, still thinking of other things, investigated various rents in his neat garments by seeing how many fingers he could stick through them. The average appeared to be four. . . .

There is a fascination about watching, through a telescope, or a peep-hole, or a printed page, the actions of a man who considers himself to be utterly alone—a fascination not dependent, either, on the age-old hope of "getting something on him." Five minutes of such occupation will prove conclusively that all that prevents most men from being excellent fellows, is the desire to appear to advantage in the eyes which, they feel, are continually watching them. They accordingly become pompous, or exaggeratedly at their ease; they smile when there is nothing to smile at, look grave when they want to grin, embellish their remarks with unspontaneous action, and, in politeness to the remarks of others, register emotions the real feeling of which, under the circumstances, would stamp them as idiots. Thus, in society, an explorer just returned from among the head-hunters of Borneo, has been seen to quake with terror at a maiden lady's account of a dog-fight; and, conversely, a prime minister of England has been watched, through a key-hole, at the urgent national business of balancing a ruler on his nose. And he did it with quite ministerial gravity. However—the fascination palls.

So it is probably time to remark, that having breakfasted, John Arnold rode back to Circle R, and, within five minutes of his arrival, was busily exercising his company manners for the benefit of Sloan and the other punchers. He was not sufficiently insane to imagine that the ranch force had the slightest intention of accepting him as foreman; yet, with their eyes upon him, he felt constrained to issue his first orders in the tone of one who takes obedience for granted.

THE SAGE HEN

"I want you boys," he said, his peculiar young-old gaze full on Sloan's face, "to put in to-day building a kind of barricade between the house and the bunk-house here, and the bunk-house and the barn, and the barn and the house. That'll make a kind of triangle.—At least, I want half of you to fly at that. The other half's coming out with me, and see if there's any cattle left on this ranch."

"Oh, we are, are they?" asked Mr. Sloan aristocratically.

John Arnold slipped out of his saddle.

"You talking to me?" he asked curtly.

"Yeah! And you can go plumb—"

It was later likened variously to the striking of a thunderbolt, the explosion of ten sticks of forty-per-cent. dynamite, and a head-on collision between two flashes of lightning. With a fresh spontaneity which negatived entirely the idea that he had been in two desperate fights in the previous twenty-four hours, John Arnold went into action again with an all-embracing fury that might have dismayed regular troops. He happened to hit Sloan a conventional, though unconventionally powerful, punch on the nose; but he seemed perfectly willing to kick, wrestle, bite, or use a gun butt—though he did none of these things, except to Pinky Pawson, who picked up a bottle, and was promptly awarded all four.

"Had enough?" snapped the terror, as Pinky fell.

"I—" began Corliss.

It was an explanatory, apologetic, rather wondering start to a conciliatory speech; but it was misinterpreted, as Corliss' remarks were rather apt to be, and Arnold stopped it with a really shocking left to the jaw.

"Anybody else?" he demanded.

There was a silence, broken only by the attempts of Mr. Sloan to breathe through the fallen arches of his nose. On either side of the hand which covered this member, a pair of mild blue eyes, still gushing involuntary tears, stared fixedly at the new foreman. As has been hinted, Mr. Sloan's mind was not of the most agile; and, tucked away in his cortical convolutions, where it had lain undisturbed since McGuffey's First Reader had put it there in 1898, was the precept that right is might—or anyway, that a good fist-fighter can't be all bad. On either side of Mr. Sloan, as he wrestled with this doctrine, the other punchers of the Circle R stood motionless and speechless because they really did not know what to do next. None of them craved the fate of Pinky Pawson for himself; but, to do them justice, it must be said that their difference arose mainly from another consideration. Sloan had been their boss; under his orders, they would have attacked this strange guy, and demolished him. But— the strange guy had demolished Sloan, and— Well, the situation was peculiar. Looked as though he was the boss himself, after that.

"I want you boys to listen to me for one minute," said John Arnold, watching them carefully, "and after that, you can come on if you like. Right at this minute, I don't want to hurt you—you look all right to me. But if you rush me after I've talked, I'll know you're a stupid bunch of louts, and it'll give me real pleasure to wipe the floor with the gang of you. Yes. Now listen. I hired out to the I. B. C. for my own reasons, which are no darn business of yours. I'm a fighter by trade. Yes— professional bad man, if you like. That's why they hired me. You-all seem to have been too tough a nut for their amateurs to crack; so they've cleaned out all the gang that was here last year, and replaced 'em with—us. Now, you boys are willing performers, but you're not trained. I am—and I'm ready to teach you. That I figured to go on the other side doesn't matter. I'm here now, and I'm no traitor. Somebody hinted last night that I was. Anybody care to say it now?"

Nobody did. Mr. Sloan, getting to his feet, and receiving a lightning stare from those strange old eyes, felt moved to utter a muffled, "Oh, no! Not me!"

"All right. 'Course, it's not nice for you to have a guy you don't like, despise, and all that, giving you orders; but it seems to me that's a dislike you might swallow for the sake of your boss. I tell you—and I don't lie—that with me in command, you've got one chance in about ten million to hold out. If you chase me out, or give me the horse laugh, the Circle R will be I. B. C. land before the end of the week."

He reached for the makings, and, as he rolled, looked, smiling, at the men around him.

"That's all," he added, snapping the match in volplaning curves through the air. "Suit yourselves."

"You—won't—sell us out?" asked Mr. Sloan doubtfully.

THE SAGE HEN

A slow flush crawled up John Arnold's cheeks; then, dropping his hand from the gun butt on which it had rested, he laughed.

"Get a new nose, and then ask me that again," he advised.

The hand which had covered the ruin was suddenly extended. It was red and sticky, but Arnold grasped it with an eagerness he did not trouble to conceal.

"Want me to build fence—or come with you?" asked the ex-foreman.

"With me," said his successor. "And will you tell off the best fence men for the barricade?"

CHAPTER VII

WITHIN ten minutes, one half of the pathetic garrison which aimed to hold Circle R against the powers of hundreds of men and millions of dollars, was busy on its defenses; while the other half, too scant in numbers to handle even a good-sized night herd, was riding forth undauntedly to subject the thousands of acres of ranch land to the processes of the spring round-up.

The expedition was, of course, a mere farce, as Mr. Sloan, during the first mile, took occasion to point out.

"I know it," replied John Arnold.

They rode on in silence. In roll after roll of gray-green grass land, the Circle R unfolded itself before them.

It was not what would have appealed to the connoisseur of Naboth's vineyards as an ideal example of the class. As scenery it was painfully monotonous; as a fenced cattle range it was, in the words of

Sloan, a mighty fine open-range proposition; and, furthermore, it showed here, there and everywhere, the signs of a year's neglect. Last spring and summer had been periods of open warfare, resulting in the loss of Old Boss Bruce and his son. Autumn had found the ranch disorganized, undermanned, and rather puzzled whether or not to take Joan Bruce seriously. Winter, especially under the shadow of a very sketchy armistice, is no time for reclamation work. So the stretch of land was getting on very nicely with the process of returning to the wilderness from which the most desperate efforts of two generations of Bruces had only succeeded in lifting it a little. The fences were falling; the loco luxuriating.

"I don't see any beeves, much," remarked John Arnold, on the crest of the sixth or seventh rise.

Sloan laughed bitterly.

"You don't tell me you expected to?" he asked. "Why, man, whatju think these I. B. C. goofs have been doin' all winter? Stealin' our cattle, of course. We're 'way behind in our brandin', naturally; an' if we weren't, a brand or so wouldn't worry them, when they can make a runnin' iron for five cents."

"Didn't you try to stop 'em?"

"Some," said Mr. Sloan laconically. "Tried to stop 'em last summer—lost twelve men an' both our bosses."

"Quit after that?"

"Say, mister. There's a live-oak over there. Look at it. That big limb. There's a rope hangin' from it still. There used to be a man on the end of that rope, but he seems to have melted away. . . . No, we didn't entirely quit; but half a dozen men can't do much guardin' on a place of this size."

They were passing under the great limb of the live-oak. The men behind the leaders swerved apart to avoid the touch of the dangling riata. A pony stumbled over a long white something that clinked like a note on a xylophone.

Arnold shuddered violently.

"Don't like it?" asked Sloan, smiling.

The melancholy eyes turned on him.

"I've been too near it myself, once or twice," said the new foreman.

With unusual vivacity, the man on his right endeavored to change the subject.

"We thought, at the time," he remarked, "that that guy deserved it better'n most anybody; an' it's

THE SAGE HEN

only because—Miss Joan 'd have taken the hide off us if she'd known about it, that he didn't get worse'n hanging. We thought we'd got the jasper that killed young Bruce—answered to his description. But that ain't much to go by. You'd answer the description as good as he did—so would Corliss yonder, barring his lamps. He said he wasn't, an' couple weeks later we found he was tellin' the truth. However, he was rustlin'. No doubt of that. Funny, though. We caught him right where Bruce must ha' got killed."

Arnold looked straight ahead.

"Is that," he asked, with a rather unexpected lightsomeness, "a cow I see before me in the distance, its tail toward my hand?"

"It's a red bull, with one eye hurt," volunteered Corliss proudly from behind.

"We're gettin' into a bunch of gulleys soon," said Sloan. "Spurs off the hills, you know. May have a few cattle been in there, where they wouldn't be found. . . . Say, do you know about how young Bruce got killed?"

After a considerable pause, Arnold shook his head; then, as if undecided, nodded it.

THE SAGE HEN

"I've heard—a good deal about it," he said constrainedly.

"Yeah—from the I. B. C. people, likely," growled the big puncher. "Now listen to this, mister, an' if it don't make you a hundred per cent. ours—"

"I thought we'd agreed I was that already?"

Sloan glanced sidewise, and was alarmed.

"Say, buddy," he protested, "don't be so all-fired quick on the trigger. I'm not nickin' you. How'm I goin' to talk if you're goin' to flare up all the time, an' go pale on me that way? If I didn't think you was all right, I wouldn't be here—no, an' you could of kept on flattenin' my nose till it stuck out of the back of my head, so chew on that. I only aim to feed you a little raw meat; but, gee, if you're goin' to bite me while I do it, you can—"

"All right. Go ahead, then."

Sloan collected his faculties.

"Well, you see," he began, "this is the way it was. An' say—you don't seem to curse much yourself, but when I tell anybody this tale, I do, an' I can't help it. We heard the I. B. C. folks were rustlin' our stock, an' so old man Bruce an' Jim Bruce an' the rest of the bunch on-saddled and started to see

THE SAGE HEN

what about it. No, that ain't the beginnin' of it, either. 'Bout six months before that, before me or any of the bunch that's here now, was on the ranch, Jim Bruce picked up a guy that was down, out, an' drinkin', in Hurst Seat—feller said his name was Haynes, an' that he was just out of Leavenworth for train-ticklin'. Claimed to be hell-bound, with no return ticket. Jim gave 'm a job on the Circle R, an' got so stuck on him, the way he talked about gratitude an' all, that when this I. B. C. trouble came up, it was Haynes he sent out to kind of scout around the other ranches in the county, an' see what was brewin'. Kind of soft, Jim was; more like his sister than his dad. Well, this here Haynes went, an' he disappeared, an' he never come back; an' ol' man Bruce, says he, 'He's flew the coop, Jimmy,' an' Jimmy, he says, 'No, sir. I treated him decently, an' he'll treat me the same way.' 'All done by kindness, eh?' says ol' man Bruce. 'As you say, sir,' says Jim. 'As I say my left foot!' sneers the old man; an' he was—right, an' may that —— of a —— of a —— Haynes flame in the everlastin' brimstone of ——"

"Whoa!" said Arnold.

91

"I can't help it. . . . Seem to be quite a lot of cows down there. What goin' to do with 'em?"

"I don't know. Might drive 'em back to that corral near the house—you know."

"Can't ship any. Railroad won't take 'em." Sloan took a reflective chew of tobacco.

"There's another railroad about twenty miles the other side of this," said Arnold; and then suddenly: "I—isn't there?"

"Thirty. Longhorn City. Couldn't drive 'em there without a whole lot more fightin' men than we've got, though. This county's solid I. B. C., mister."

Arnold considered.

"M'm. Well, go on with the story. Sorry I butted in."

"It'd take five hundred head to make it worth while," said Sloan; who had his own crude ideas about the technique of suspense, "an' what with them bein' so wild, mister, I dunno whether we could herd 'em back. 'Course, we could bring the rest of the boys out to-morrow an' have a shot at it, but it's a long way—"

"Have to be done to-day if at all," snapped

THE SAGE HEN

Arnold. "The I. B. C.'s opening their spring campaign, don't forget. One day's liable to make the difference between whether we find some cattle, or none. . . . What's that?"

Over the landscape there had brooded a vast empty silence whose completeness was not impaired by the sounds of the advancing horses. The soft thud-thud of hoofs on short grass, the creak and strain of cinches and saddles, the occasional clink of a stirrup or buck hook against a buckle, the rattle of spurs, were silence to these men who spent their lives ahorse, just as the roar of trains, the rumble of wagons, the whine of elevators, and the thud of footsteps over his head, are, from long usage, inaudible to the city dweller. But as the faintest new addition to the grand chorus of New York cacaphony will strike the hardened flat inhabitant as a noise, so did the small sound as of something dropped in the blue-domed immensity of the prairie, cause the cavalcade to halt, listen and analyze.

"Shootin'?" asked Sloan.

The distant "spat" sounded again, its sharp note burdened now, to the more careful ear, with a tiny undertone that deepened it.

"It is shootin'," said one of the men. "Rifle."

Arnold drew his Winchester from its scabbard, glanced at the dented stock, remembered the plugged muzzle, and slipped it back again.

"Look—look," cried Corliss suddenly. "Up there on the butte. The guy that was shootin's got up. We're outa range from there."

"We ain't *all* telescopes," snapped Sloan. "Where is he—what is he?"

"Why, dog bite my ear off, it's a nigger. He's shakin' his fist. Can't you see him? Now he's off—he's outa sight. Say—"

Arnold turned around in his saddle. His face was pale and set.

"Listen, boys," he said, "that means we'll have to get those beeves away to-day—if there's enough of them to make it worth while. That coon was one of the bunch that tried to kidnap Miss Joan last night. I laid him kicking, but he's come to, apparently. Now he's either been shooting our stock from the top of that butte, or scouting 'em out, so that a gang can come drive them."

"Phew!" said Sloan, pushing his hat over his eyes and scratching the back of his head as he surveyed

THE SAGE HEN

the distant stock. "That'll be some day's work, buddy, take it from me!"

"If you don't want to try it," said Arnold slowly, "I can't make you."

"Who said I didn't want to try it? Just as soon be trampled to death as go any other way. You boys would too, wouldn'tcha? Say no, an' I'll punch the livers out of you."

"It'll be fun," said Corliss sadly.

"There's five of us here. One at each corner and one for boss rider—we ought to do it. It's no larger than a good many beef cuts."

"But, oh, so much wilder!" said Sloan. "I suppose you want to ride boss?"

"I don't want to shirk it."

There was a scarcely audible grunt of approval. If anything went wrong; if the herd, once started toward its corral, should suddenly decide that, having enjoyed its freedom so long, it would not submit to human domination in this instance, there would be trouble for all, but certain death for the leader of the herd, riding ahead, right in the path of the stampede. It was fairly obvious to the experts that this man with the old eyes was not a cattle man;

though, being in Texas, he certainly knew the perils menacing even the most hardened and experienced of boss riders in a drive. In accepting, as he was not compelled to, the risk attached to his foremanship, Arnold was acting as the four men with him had begun, since his behavior of that morning, to expect that he would. And nothing gratifies humanity so much as having its expectations fulfilled. It gives it a chance to utter the sweetest phrase in the language—which is, undoubtedly—"I told you so!"

"Well, we'll see about that, when an' if we get the damn animals together," growled Sloan. The cavalcade moved forward again. "Say, it's funny—everything seems to remind me of that tale I was tellin' you. That sniper on the butte, f'r instance."

"Yes?"

"Say, don't you want me to tell you this story?"

Arnold turned and grinned; yet there was an expression on his face which Mr. Sloan wrestled to interpret during a goodly portion of his ensuing narrative. A very strange look. Probably the guy was thinking how the hoofs would feel in his back, if anything went wrong—no, that wasn't it. Looked as if something was hurting him, though.

"Fire ahead," was what he said, however; and Mr. Sloan did so.

"Well—as I was sayin'—we rode out, old man Bruce, an' young Jimmy, an' the rest of us, to where we heard these I. B. C. thieves were rustling our stock—back there, just this side of that big hump in the ground, where the live-oak is. Got about two hundred yards away from it, goin' quiet, so's not to disturb anybody, when *walloomp* goes a rifle from right by the oak's roots, an' a guy called Petersen says, 'A-a-ah!' an' falls sideways off his horse. He was ridin' alongside of young Jimmy, an' there's no doubt that bullet was intended for Jim, because the next one took old man Bruce in the throat, an' the next one after that flipped the brains outa the foreman. Say, whoever was doin' that snipin' had a quick hand on the magazine slide, an' a dirty eye for a bead. An' he knew who was who on the Circle R, too. Three shots, an' two-thirds of the officers down. 'Course, we fanned out then, old man Bruce, still in his saddle, tryin' to shout orders about somethin'. He was a game old devil, that one. Cripes, it was terrifyin'. There was no use tryin' to shoot the sniper—

couldn't see him; an' the moment anybody'd start to ride him down, that guy would check out. Well, I'd just started a rush, an' got a bullet along my scalp, when I see young Jim, who'd been kind of milling around near his dad, suddenly pull his pony sideways an' start off at the devils' own gallop—back home. Well, sir, I caught a glimpse of his face, an' it was as white as a sheet, an' his eyes starin', an' wet runnin' out of the corners of his mouth an' *I* thought he was runnin' away. As for old man Bruce, when he saw it, he just loosed everything an' fell off his horse. Doc Brewer said, with his throat all shot to pieces the way it was, he couldn't possibly have whispered, even; but I'm goin' to swear to you, mister, that when he seen his son turn around an' beat it, the old chap gave a regular scream—like a shot horse, I'd say; an' when we carried him back to the ranch house, his lips kept movin', kind of weak, like he was sayin' some one word, over and over again. Nobody could make anythin' outa it; but I've thought it over since, an' I think he was sayin', 'Coward! Coward! Coward!' See, his family settled this district, an' fought in everythin' there was goin', an'—well, you see."

THE SAGE HEN

"There's a whole bunch of steers in that coulee, there, boss," called Corliss. "Gee, there must be a thous—"

"You shut up," snarled the narrator over his shoulder. If thoughts could kill, some of the most ferocious murders in the history of crime would lie to the account of tale-tellers, interrupted at the Glory Be.

"Well, sir," continued Sloan, grasping at his tattered passion, "the old man had been a square guy all his life, an' I guess that's why God let him live another twenty-four hours, in spite of Doc Brewer's sayin' he couldn't survive the night, because at about six o'clock the next day, a line rider from the Stony Springs outfit come over—the Stony Springs hadn't gone over to the I. B. C. yet—an' he'd bin to Hurst Seat that afternoon. An' while he was there, he'd seen a feller ravin' about the town, all drunk, shoutin' that he was the bad wild man from Borneo, an' that he'd fixed young Bruce's clock. 'Try to take us in the flank, would he?' shouts the feller. 'Well, where is he now? I showed him how the Indians fight, I did!' Seems he was wavin' a knife as he said it, an' finally the sheriff took an'

THE SAGE HEN

locked him up. Not for murder—oh, no. He was an I. B. C. man. For disorderly conduct. An' the Stony Springs puncher went an' saw him in the lock-up, an' this jasper told him all about it, shriekin' an' laughin' an' boastin' in his cell. Seems he'd been with the rustlin' party that was finishin' its work while this sniper guy held us back. Well, young Bruce hadn't run away at all—he'd just done what none of us had the brains to do. That white look on his face was rage an' what-not, an' he'd swung a circle around an' gone to take that sniper in the rear. But this guy'd seen him comin' an' when poor little Jimmy crep up near the live-oak, he got a bullet in the heart. 'An' I cut his throat an' scalped him, too,' yells the drunk. 'As sure as my name's Haynes, I took his hair!' 'I'll take yours, in another minute,' says the Stony Springs puncher. 'Not while he's my prisoner, you won't,' says the sheriff. 'Maybe he won't be your prisoner long,' says the Stony Springs man, ridin' off to tell us boys. An' of course, that was the sheriff's excuse for lettin' the skunk out that night. Pretended to transfer him to another jail—an' accidentally let him escape.

THE SAGE HEN

"Well, you heard me tell how the killer said '—sure as my name's Haynes.' When we heard that, us all standing around in the room where old man Bruce was dyin', we give a yell that shook the ranch house; but the old man didn't care about any Haynes. All he could understand, all he cared about, was that his boy hadn't run away after all, but had been killed in action. Mister, I tell you that when he heard about his own son bein'—bein' all hackled up like that, the old man's eyes fairly lit up with joy. It was too much for him; because he tried to speak, an' he choked, an' then—he was dead, sm-sm-smilin'!"

"Who the hell's cryin'?" demanded Corliss indignantly from behind. "I was lullookin' at the beeves an' some a-a-ash got into my eye!"

Sloan, unashamed, wiped tears off his cheeks with the flat palms of his hands.

"I don't give a damn," he said defiantly, "I always blubber when I tell that story; an' if I ever catch the —— —— —— that it's about, I'll give him something to —— —— Well —— cry for— an' no —— —— eyes to cry with, the —— —— Say, mister, do you expect us to punch that collec-

THE SAGE HEN

tion of meat? Look at the blighters! There's millions of them. An' all fit for the bull-ring. Gosh, look at that longhorn yonder, moppin' at us!"

Without further words, the cutting out began.

There was not a man of the five but had had his experiences of hardship, winter and summer on the range—it was to be seen, as soon as the cut began, that Arnold, though lacking the finished technique born of long continuous practise, had punched cows at some time in his career. And, to continue the first phrase—there was not a man of the five but admitted when at last a ragged herd was on the move, that this struggle in the shadow of the foothills surpassed anything of which he had dreamed in his wildest nightmare.

Not that it was at all spectacular, save at isolated moments, as when Corliss' pony, scuttling to head off a stampeding bunch, stepped in a gopher hole and flung his rider straight in the path of the advancing steers. Then it was Sloan who, with both guns going, and with vocal bellows enough to wake the dead, managed to swerve the stampede the few feet which saved the telescopic gentleman's life. Arnold and the other three men were up coulees, choking in the dust which made their ponies' lather into mud, engaged in the monotonous yet perilous task of driving out cattle not accustomed to be driven, quite satisfied where they were, and possessed with a fiendish determination, once they had been dislodged, to slip back, past the cursing man and cavorting pony in the dust cloud, back to their old grazing ground.

The work started at eleven in the morning; and, to be briefer than the subject deserves, continued without interruption until nearly five in the afternoon. There was no stop for food, because there was no food. Each man had water in his canteen—lukewarm water, full of dust, which he drank sparingly, ahorse. To stop for rest was impossible—even a few minutes' relaxation of watchfulness over that quicksilver-like herd would have undone the work of hours. And the net result of all the torture the five had undergone—thirst, choking, semi-blindness from the constant watching of milling beeves in the bright light—was disappointing. One man could work a coulee fairly well; but for two men, however expert, to bunch and handle the strays as they came lolloping, charging or slinking into the

THE SAGE HEN

open, in ones, twos, fives, dozens, wild and ferocious, was impossible. Largely by good luck, however, the first reddening of the sun found a bunch of seven or eight hundred head fairly close together; upon which Sloan, firing three shots rapidly in the air, followed by a second three, summoned the men from the draws, and gave the order to "tuck 'em in."

When the stragglers had been pushed into formation, and the whole herd bullied into a shambling, irregular movement in the general direction of the Circle R corral, he dropped back from his position at the head of the column, to where Arnold, haggard with fatigue, was riding flank, and abruptly suggested a swap of positions.

"You better get up ahead, mister," he gasped hoarsely, "if I know cows, this lot's goin' to spread rather'n stampede. Don't let your hawse fall down, though. Try breathin' through your handkerchief in another place—it's solid mud where you got it now. Ah, would you, you—?"

He was off to try unconventional methods—to-wit, a shocking punch in the eye—on a young steer who was endeavoring to leave the ranks.

THE SAGE HEN

"Git up ahead, or they'll be away from us!" his voice came back faintly, as he spurred farther down the cloud-enveloped herd to rowel his right spur against the nose of another aspirant for liberty.

So they proceeded, through what seemed like interminable miles of flat lands, sage-brush, and dust—dust—dust. It was only the same distance as they had cheerfully ridden out that morning; but to the exhausted men, the earth under their ponies' feet seemed like a treadmill; the journey endless. They were nervously tired out, really hysterical, though they showed none of the conventional signs of the condition, and it would have been a bold man, with no sense of humor, who would have offered the rabid, sweat-streaked, cursing Sloan or his lieutenants, burnt feathers or sal volatile in water. Though a burnt cigar and a few fingers of Bourbon would have been welcome. . . . Mr. Sloan, in fact, thought of the Bourbon as a retreating beef kicked an ounce or two of alkali into his windpassages, decided that it would be the cure for his ills, remembered prohibition, and groaned aloud. That a man of his former habits could forget, even temporarily, such a feature of our national life, tells

THE SAGE HEN

more as to his mental condition than several pages of purely medical symptoms. . . .

Even purgatory, however, is subject to the operation of time; and at last—at long last—the voice of Corliss, cracked and wavering, rose in a dismal howl which announced approaching relief from torment. For a moment, from the brow of the hillock on which stood the live-oak with its dangling rope, the Circle R ranch house hove in sight, to be instantly swallowed up, with its barns and its inviting corral, as the herd swooped down the slope.

"Speed 'em up!" yelled Sloan, at the foot of the next ascent.

Like the other men, he was probably hungry for another glimpse of the building which marked the goal of this excessively fool enterprise, of which, in his heart, he was prouder than of anything save his capture of the bucking belt at Longhorn City in '08. But his order had a more important purpose. Cattle, like the two-legged varieties of fauna, will go into things when excited, which their cooler judgment would cause them to avoid; and in Mr. Sloan's opinion, a wild bunch like this would regularly need stampeding into the corral—whose bars, he earnestly prayed, would be let down in time by the fence-building garrison of the ranch. If not, there would be beef jelly in plenty, without the assistance of a factory. However, that was no concern of his.

"Ready, mister?" he howled at Arnold's back, and saw an arm raised in assent. "Then whoop 'em up this hill, boys! Hi-ya! Start 'em rollin'! Roll them tails, an' roll 'em high. We'll a-a-all be angels by and by-y-y-y-y! Get back, you —— —— —— cow, you! Hi-ya-a-a! Shoot 'em up! Hi-yip!"

With undignified haste, and with a conglomerate expression of earnest viciousness, the herd changed step, and, as it surmounted the crest of the undulation, the rear ranks were shoving and shouldering the bovine leaders.

"Look out!" yelled Sloan, "you in the lead! Shake your dogs! They're climbin'!"

The first symptom of the grand rush that was to end in the corral, merged into the second as the front of the herd, snorting, bellowing, and rolling its tails as requested by the flank rider, put on speed and drew away from the rear ranks. For a moment, there was a gap between the two sections; then it closed, and the herd thundered forward as a whole.

"Hi-yi-yip! Get back, you son of perdition. Hey, you in the lead, you—"

For the first few moments after the swing over the last hill brow, Sloan had been watching his flank, prepared to stimulate or repress as occasion should demand. Now he turned his face forward to see how John Arnold was making out.

He gave a gasp of horror, which, an instant later he dimly heard echoed from behind him by three shouts of dismay and warning.

"Look after the herd!" Sloan yelled at the top of his voice, scarcely knowing what he said; and himself, with the automatic action of a man thoroughly versed in his job, spurred forward to take Arnold's place in the van.

CHAPTER XVIII

WHAT Sloan had seen was this:
Five hundred yards away, there was riding toward them a cavalcade of perhaps a dozen men, spread out behind a leader. Ahead of this cavalcade, fleeing from it with three hundred yards' start, Joan Bruce had been riding, when her horse stumbled. Now, while the animal struggled to regain its feet, she lay still, straight in the path of the stampeding herd which, as John Arnold spurred his pony forward to her rescue, put on speed and followed its leader at a terrifying gallop.

"Work 'em over to the left!" shrieked Sloan, driving his left spur desperately into the eye of the beef on the right forward corner of the flying herd.

He glanced ahead again, before, with lightning motion, he dropped hand to his belt and drew the gun not discharged in recalling the rounders-up. Arnold was half-way to the girl, and starting to bend over in his saddle, as if to attempt snatching

THE SAGE HEN

her up from the ground. That would pull his arms out of their sockets, and they would both be trampled to death. The maddened herd was gaining on the staggering weary horse.

Taking a desperate chance, Sloan jammed the muzzle of his revolver against a steer's forehead and fired. The animal, stumbling on its knees and rolling sidewise, nearly cut the feet from under his pony; but, after a moment's eddying and bellowing about the writhing carcass, the herd swung away from the obstruction, ever so little to the left. Too desperate to rejoice, Sloan fired again; but not with the same result. This time, he did not kill; and the infuriated steer, swerving its rush with incredible agility, was on him. He fired again, and the brute dropped its head, fell to its knees, and blundered against the killer's pony. Horse and man rolled in the dust.

The herd, in a frenzy, even increased its speed; and at this moment, when the thundering hoofs which in all probability would chop him to pieces, were a bare thirty yards behind him, Arnold grabbed for the Sage Hen's belt. There was every chance in the world that Jinny, foot-weary and staggering, would strike her hoof on that auburn head, which was almost under her belly as her master reached for his grip; there was every chance that the slim belt, designed to support a light gun and a couple of dozen cartridges, would snap; it seemed impossible that the eye, arm and leg-muscles of any man could bring off the miracle of cooperation necessary for this rescue. Yet they did—and the hoofs missed, and the belt held. Jinny felt a sudden weight added to her burden, her cinches twisted agonizingly by a strange one-sided force; something heavy and limp and brushing against her knees.

Then, almost in the same instant it seemed, the usually gentle hand of her master jammed the bit cruelly back and to the right, so that she perforce sunfished in her own length; the spurs were driven horribly into her sides, so that she leaped forward like a cat in torture; and then—something blunt and irresistible cannoned against her shoulder, knocking her clear off her feet. There was a smother of dust; rolling over and over in which, the little pony remembered, while wondering if this was the end of the equine world, that in a fall such as this, she must by no means lash out with her hoofs.

THE SAGE HEN

John Arnold had won out by just that fraction of a second in which a fast pony, hard-spurred, can cover the distance between a steer's breast and shoulder. The herd, led by the right flank steer which had spilled Jinny and her burdens, thundered away past the corral and the ranch house, toward the boundaries of the I. B. C.'s subsidiary, the Lazy F.

They were lost and gone for ever, quite as certainly as was anybody's darling Clementine since the beginning of the world; and if King Solomon had been in Arnold's place, he would probably have needed some little time to decide whether to curse and shake his royal fist after them, or to go down on his devout knees and return thanks. For the time being, however, the leader of the stampede was beyond doubt or questioning.

Sloan and the three other punchers, sweating and dust-whitened, rode up simultaneously with the men who had been chasing Joan Bruce, to find Arnold lying with his arms flung out to protect the head of the awakening girl—quite unconscious and, though they did not know it, dreaming—

Strange dreams, such as one experiences only in

THE SAGE HEN

a faint, in a coma, or following the keen cold whiff of ether; strange choking dreams of bondage—of a little cell—not enough air—and dark, very dark; with a strange, close smell. There ought to have been light shining through the little barred window, high up in the wall—there ought to have been sounds from the other cells. Yes,—there was somebody banging his door; no, that was the blood in his ears. And the bed—he was lying on the bed; it was hard and lumpy. Why couldn't he feel the rasp of the coarse blanket, with its flecks of fiber sticking out like bristles from the wool? It must be morning soon. Then the light would come through the window. But there ought to be a star visible, even at night, or a patch of sky, lighter against the darkness. . . . Where was the window? This wasn't his own cell. He was in a strange place—a strange cell—why, in God's name, wouldn't it get light?

"Steady, steady!" came a voice from a great distance.

That was the warder . . . now the light was breaking. Oh God, to be out and free. . . .

He made a violent effort and sat up.

"Take it easy," said the voice, now close at hand. "Steady, now. Plenty of time."

"That's him," said another voice.

Arnold saw a circle of dim figures around him, tried to rise, and with the aid of an arm behind him, accomplished the feat. Suddenly his eyes snapped back into focus. Who were these ugly-looking jaspers in front of him? There was Sloan and the other two boys. Corliss was holding him up. He smiled at Joan Bruce, and then suddenly stopped smiling. His eyes had fallen on the left breast of the coat of the man nearest him.

A sheriff's star.

"Hello!" said Arnold unsteadily.

"Hello," said the sheriff. "What's your name?"

There was a silence.

Sloan broke it. His usually ruddy face was pale and set; the big knotted hand resting on the butt of his right-hand gun trembled. His lips, even, were unsteady; his eyes blazed.

"Buddy," he said slowly, "I don't believe it about you—not if this guy here identified you a thousand times. He's gone over to the I. B. C. himself, with the rest of the Stony Springs outfit—"

THE SAGE HEN

"You sneer at me—" began the tall lean man who had said "That's him!"

"Shut up," said the sheriff.

Sloan turned on him.

"You tell *me* to shut up, you yellow-backed coyote," he said through his teeth, "an' I'll take an' ram your star down your throat, posse or no posse. If you're here on the straight, you ain't necessary. The Circle R can look after its own business. An' if you're here to frame this guy up, look out! . . . Buddy, I kind o' took a fancy to you. For God's sake tell me you ain't what he says you are. For if you are, by the Almighty, I'll spatter your brains where you stand."

"What's that?" asked Arnold. Suddenly, the melancholy eyes had begun to wander. Jinny was perhaps five yards away, standing with bowed head, yet with eyes brightened by her twenty minutes of rest and of rolling, as well as she could for her saddle, in the sand. And the sun was well down on the horizon. Half an hour more, and the day would have shaded abruptly into the semi-tropical night.

"What's that?" he repeated.

Sloan opened his mouth, then turned to the sheriff.

THE SAGE HEN

"You can tell him!" he roared. "It's your dirty job, not mine."

"Your name is John Arnold?"

"Yes."

"Formerly known as Midge Carlton, Sad Jim Connery, and *Walter Haynes?*"

There was an appalling silence.

"Released after two years' imprisonment in Leavenworth Penitentiary, for train-robbing, under the name of *Walter Haynes?*"

No answer.

"For the love of God—" began Sloan hoarsely. Behind him, the Sage Hen, white as a sheet, clasped her hands.

"What's the use of all this?" demanded the lean puncher from Stony Springs. "I tell you I know him. He's the guy I seen in Hurst Seat jail, tellin' about how he scalped—"

Joan Bruce gave a faint scream.

"You shut up," said Sloan to the lean man.

The sheriff, one hand at his belt, the other coming out of a pocket above whose edge showed an ominous corner of legal blue paper, began to speak slowly:

THE SAGE HEN

"Assuming you to be the person mentioned in this warrant, I arrest you—"

"Arnold!" cried Joan Bruce, pushing forward.

The big man with the sad eyes looked at her.

The girl glanced quickly around the circle which enclosed them. Her hair, loose, flowed over her shoulders; her eyes were wide, her cheeks flushed. Under the torn khaki of her riding-dress, her bosom fluttered rapidly.

"Arnold—you've saved my life; I don't believe what this man has been saying about you. I don't believe you're the traitor that killed my brother. If you say it's untrue, we shall not let him take you. I think it is a trick to rob us of another man. I have said I would never fight the law in this business; but if this is the law, I will fight it!"

Sloan and Corliss growled. The other punchers from the Circle R—the fence-builders, who had joined the gathering around the unconscious form of John Arnold, and who now stood, by strange coincidence, each next to a man of the sheriff's posse—moved uneasily. There was a faint, pervasive rattle of steel against leather—the steel of gun barrels against the cowhide of holsters.

"This is no business for women," growled the sheriff, stepping forward.

"You'll find it is," blazed Joan Bruce.

The peace officer's eyes had been searching Arnold's face.

"All right," he said. "Let's see what you've got. On information received, that you are the person named in this warrant, I arrest you, Walter Haynes, alias John Arnold, for the wilful murder of James Bruce."

A silence.

"Say something!" croaked Sloan out of a dry throat. "Say you ain't him! For God's sake, say it!"

Again Arnold glanced about him.

"Why should I say that?" he asked, in a strange quiet voice. "I am Walter Haynes!"

Sloan's hand, paralyzed, did not move on his gun butt. "Then you didn't kill him!" he whispered. "Say that, an' we'll clean 'em up. After—after he'd befriended you! You couldn't!"

"I did."

"You're trying to save us—the fight," said Joan Bruce, shrinking. "Upon your oath—"

THE SAGE HEN

They saw Arnold's teeth sink into his lip.

"Upon my honor—" he said; and, turning, seemed to hold out his wrists for the handcuffs.

Only seemed to do so, however; because, before Sloan, with a bellow of rage, could pull his gun; before the sheriff could so much as reach for the polished steel bracelets at his belt, the humble outstretching of those powerful arms had changed into a hungry clutch which seized the sheriff by the waist, wrenched him off his feet, and hurled him, broadside on, to knock Sloan and the other three men flying. Another man who had drawn a gun felt his senses detonate and leave him, as a fist drove his jaw backward and up.

Then, scrambling for his seat on Jinny, spurring hard, regardless of the shots which whined over him, John Arnold fled into the gathering dusk.

There were three events worthy of note, during what remained of the second twenty-four hours of Arnold's second sojourn in the United States:

The posse followed him until the darkness covered him, and he was lost in the mazes of the Hurst County hills.

At ten o'clock, an unknown mob, headed by a

gigantic negro who sang a horrible song at the top of his voice, attacked the Circle R ranch house, and was beaten off from the half-finished barricade with the loss of two dead and one wounded. Joan Bruce fought by the side of her men. Sloan, at every shot into the hostile darkness, gritted through his teeth, "That's for you, Haynes!"

David Grant, riding from Hurst Seat, where he had heard rumors, to the assistance of the garrison, met the returning posse a mile from where the battle was quite audibly raging and, arrested for an imaginary, projected, or non-existent disturbance of the peace, was handcuffed, fettered and locked in the Hurst Seat jail.

One more thing—a consequence of these events.

After reports had been made to him, Mr. Rigby, in his suite at the Hurst Hotel, might have been seen to smile pleasantly, and rub his long, rather moistly sticky hands.

CHAPTER IX

MR. HENRIK IBSEN, the well-known Scandinavian dramatist, has laid it down as a law that no man in his right mind ever talks to himself; which statement, though sensational, proves nothing, except that Mr. Henrik Ibsen, the well-known Scandinavian dramatist, had never punched cattle, or been alone much under any other distressing circumstances. Had he ever, for as much as six months, abandoned the fjords where the sea-birds and the tourists scream together, and lived in Texas, he would have discovered that under conditions of real solitude, the only man who doesn't talk to himself occasionally is the chap who either hasn't enough brains to think of anything to say, or knows himself to be such a skunk that he can't bear to hear his own voice. Of course, the days when a cowpuncher would address foot-hills as "What-ho, ye everlasting mountains" and so on, are gone for ever; but it's a strange wilderness-dweller that does not chat with himself sometimes, however briefly.

THE SAGE HEN

John Arnold was positively telegraphic; but he spoke to himself nevertheless. To be exact, he sat, two hours later, on a rock high up in the Hurst County hills, stared down into the dusk which was beginning to enfold Three Pines Valley, and remarked: "Well, that's torn it."

After which he was silent, save for a sharp "Shut up!" to his pony, as she nosed among the loose stones of the hill-side in the vain hope of finding something edible.

She deserved the best of the best, that pony, after the mad scramble she'd had, with a raving, shooting, hard-riding posse at her heels, and it was not the least of John Arnold's troubles, that there was nothing for her. The fodder-bag had contained so few grains that her first eager snuffles had emptied it; and now she stood sweating, scratched, blown, and with fetlocks sore from flying pebbles—minus even a drink of water. To forage, before dark, in these hills which the pursuers knew, and the fugitive didn't, would be an almost suicidal risk.

"Wonder what that is?" Arnold demanded, just in time to cover a hurt appealing whicker from behind him.

THE SAGE HEN

The setting sun had expended its last ray on a line of bright copper wire which, after tortuous bends near the hills, ran to Three Pines, and thence cut straight away, in a bee-line for Longhorn City. It was rather strange that the man on the hill should have noticed the telephone line at that moment; for just then it was carrying a conversation of considerable interest to him. Old Bill Garfield, sitting in his International Emporium and Sheriff's Office, was, in fact, squandering thirty cents on a talk with Willie Masters, the ranger captain who made Longhorn City his headquarters.

"I think, Willie," the old gentleman was saying, "that it's high time something was done about it, and that's what!"

"What's what?"

"Whattamean?"

"I mean," said Willie Masters, who had just come in, and was being watched, with hot dull eyes, by four Mexican gentlemen in handcuffs, whom he had brought with him, "I mean, Bill, what's to be done about it? Have you any suggestions, or are you just talking for the sake of talking? Hurry! I'm sweating, and I want my supper."

THE SAGE HEN

"Well—" said Mr. Garfield, slowly.

"I may's well tell you," said Willie Masters, wiping his forehead on the transmitter, "that I've got orders to do nothing, on the ground that it's the county's business—"

"How come you got orders such as that?"

"Ask me something about Hebrew," snapped Willie, "I don't speak Greek. Ain't you got any imagination, Bill? Why have I got orders to leave the I. B. C. alone! You ask me!"

"Oh," said Mr. Garfield; and then, after a moment—"Well, good-by!"

"By!" said Mr. Masters, hanging up, and taking off his shirt.

"That's ripped it wide open, all right," said the brooding outlaw—as appositely as if he had heard the ranger captain remove Joan Bruce's last hope of legal protection. However, he was repeating his comment on his own circumstances only, and consideration of them brought into the front of his mind the still harder plight of his little mare. She had made a gallant effort to be uncomplaining; but she was all in. As her master turned from his survey of the gloaming valley so far below, and looked

124

THE SAGE HEN

at her, she drooped her muzzle against the cool surface of a rock, swaying where she stood, and began to whimper pitifully.

Arnold's hand, when he laid it on her neck, was clenched hard.

"Buck up, old lady," he said through his teeth. "Cheero, now. 'Course, if it's as bad as that, we'll have to do something. Why didn't you say so before?"

The pony whinnied and tried to toss her head as she was accustomed to do when her lord petted her. But she staggered and almost fell. Arnold, who had not the loose mouth of the habitual swearer, ripped out an appalling oath. In fear of surprise, he had left the saddle on the pony; now, drawing his knife, he cut the cinches and threw the costly burden on the ground.

"Now then, sweetie," he said. "Take a deep breath and get your legs going. There's going to be a full horse or a dead man pretty soon, one or the other. That's right—roll!"

Freed, the mare had picked out a little sandy spot and flung herself down. She rolled twice—three times, and made a lashing attempt to roll clean over;

failed, and at the fourth roll, got to her feet. She stood, mud-caked now, but obviously feeling better.

"You got a hell of a boss, leaving you saddled that way," said Arnold. "But come on. We'll do better in future."

He snapped his fingers, clicked his tongue, and started forward, the mare following him with ears pricked hopefully.

"I don't know—" the man muttered: and then stopped both speech and motion.

Far away, apparently from a spot higher up the hills, and a considerable distance south of the point at which he stood, the red glow of a fire showed against the hanging ceiling of mist and darkness.

For a whole minute, the hunted man stood motionless, staring at the faint ruddy nimbus, realizing fully what it meant to him in danger. Then the animal at his elbow sighed wearily.

Without another moment of hesitation, John Arnold started toward the fire.

CHAPTER X

IT WAS John Arnold's sincere opinion, as it would have been the opinion of any sensible man under the circumstances, that the fire was one lit by the night-riding posse, and that the men from whom he was aiming to obtain fodder and water for his horse, were the men from whom he had escaped with such difficulty. A thought made him pause in his tracks. Though he was the man whose blood the law demanded for the murder of Joan Bruce's brother, and though the sheriff of Hurst County and his posse were representatives of the law, the outlaw had not the slightest delusion that the posse's purpose was to arrest him in due form, and bring him to regular trial.

Though acting under cover of a warrant, the posse was actually moving at the orders of the International Beef Concern; the crime for which it aimed to arrest its quarry was not mere murder, but his desertion of the concern, to espouse the lost cause of Joan Bruce; and the result of such arrest would be, by the same token, not trial, but perfectly summary death by rope or bullet.

"Can't do much for her now," Arnold said in a whisper, "but I could do a whole lot less if I was dead."

He stood meditating this and staring at the distant fire, until the waiting pony whickered and nuzzled him again. Then, like an automaton, he resumed his advance.

Like most things in the mountains, the glow in the sky had seemed nearer than it was, and the intervening space of rocks, dwarf cactus, and pebbly wastes, presented obstacles which, had man or horse been just a little more exhausted, or just a little less finely mettled, would have proved insurmountable. As it was, however, an hour's steady progress brought them within a long stone's throw of the blaze. It was burning in a hollow, a cuplike depression on one of the foot-hills' minor peaks, at the foot of whose upward slope, man and horse stopped.

"Stay here," Arnold whispered, boxing the pony's nose gently to point his meaning. As he turned to

THE SAGE HEN

go, the weary animal whined in protest at the desertion; and received an admonitory smack on the muzzle that nearly knocked her off her feet.

"Quiet!" snapped the man's voice tensely.

In an instant, he was gone into the blackness of the hillside.

In ten minutes, he was lying flat behind a scrubby bush of something prickly, staring down into the hollow where the fire burned.

The men around it, a dozen in number, sat with their gun belts on as they ate; from behind each came the gleam of a rock-propped rifle; but they were emphatically not the sheriff and his posse!

Arnold's eyes examined each man in turn, looking for a face familiar through the encounter of that afternoon. For a moment, he thought he remembered the man who was tending the pot which swung over the glowing embers. Then he saw that this fellow was obviously a Mexican, with a drooping, ragged mustache and a long white scar down one cheek—a villainous-looking ruffian; at the sight of whom, the watching outlaw raised his head, and scanned the opposite rim of the depression as though looking for confirmation of an opinion suddenly formed. And, sure enough, directly across from him, squatting with rifle cradled in arms, he perceived the man he was looking for—the sentry without whom no well-organized band of bandits ever sits down to a meal.

"Is the stew done, Luis?" asked a voice in the little canyon.

Arnold craned his neck as far as he dared for fear of the sentry. Only one man in such a gathering would have the privilege of asking that question in just that tone—the acknowledged boss; and the personality—and possibly the physique—of the man who had the say-so about fodder in that company was a matter of great importance to Arnold.

The Mexican, lifting the pot cover, probed within with a pointed stick; and a pungent, spicy, hungry steam wafted into the air.

"I don't think, Meester Boss—"

"You don't think! Say, I'm hungry, boy! Let *me* think about it!"

Obligingly, the leader of this gang of obvious cutthroats stepped into the full light of the fire and probed with the pointed stick himself.

"That's done enough," he said. "Say—smells like Mexico, doesn't it?"

THE SAGE HEN

"Ow, Mexico!" came a dozen disgusted voices.

The leader made a sign that the cook should dish out the mess, his own pannikin first. As the remainder of the company, scrambling to their feet, formed a rough queue, their tin dishes clanking and glittering, he improved the shining hour with a little speech. Arnold noted its salient points, while he took in the outstanding physical characteristics of the speaker—a bull neck, a protruding jaw with two long rolls of stubble-blued fat along the jaw bones; a height of six feet or more; and an almost fantastic breadth of shoulder. The man's forehead and eyes he could not see for the brim of his hat; they were to be imagined as the brow and eyes of a not too scrupulous prize-fighter.

"You boys don't seem to like the name of Mexico," said the leader, "and I take this opportunity to tell you that, if you play your cards right, there won't be any necessity for any of you to go back there again. And by playing your cards right, I mean, listening to what I tell you to do, and doing it. Remember, I got you-all together, and I know what I got you together for. If it wasn't for me, you'd still be a bunch of soreheads hidin' in Mexico for your crimes, an' livin' on beans because you couldn't get anythin' better. Thanks to me, you're an invadin' army, livin' on the fat of the land, and on the way to make enough kale so when we break up, you can all go to some place in God's country, and live on white men's food."

The bull-necked man took a reflective spoonful of stew and surveyed his invading army.

"If anybody wants to quit now an' go back to his beans an' his solitary soreheadedness, let him say so this minute. We're really startin', from now on; an' any guy that quits after this, 'll have a bullet in the lungs for a souvenir. I'll present him with it— free of charge."

There was no answer.

"If anybody," said the big man, after another gustatory pause, "ain't satisfied with me for a leader, an' thinks he would be better in the job, let him come forward now and throw his hat where I can step on it. Because after this, the question won't be settled by plain fighting. I'll just shoot the first guy that don't obey my every last word."

There was an apologetic cough from the ranks.

"Whose side do we take in this here Hurst County war?" asked a voice. "The girl or the—"

"Nobody's!" roared the big man. "We take our own side. Ain't I told you we take our own side? We're here to grab what we can while everybody's too busy fightin' to take any notice of us! Are you deaf, or what?"

He had never let the gang so far into his confidence before, and in roaring that he had, he was employing a device very common with bosses who hold their positions by sheer force of brutality. Without a savage unreasonableness, continuously displayed and backed by threat of relentless fist and pistol, he would have had no power with that desperate bunch. And he knew his job very well. Quite obviously, he watched the effect of this outburst before repeating his vital question.

"I was askin' if anybody thought," he said, surveying the properly cowed gang, "that he had a chance to knock me kickin', and lead this expedition himself. Now's the time."

From the men before him came only the sound of the consumption of stew. Relieved, though not surprised, the bull-necked man had dipped his own spoon once more into the pottage, when from the cliff behind him, there came a clear voice:

"That offer open to all comers?"

—And to the astonished eyes of the men in the hollow, there was suddenly disclosed the figure of John Arnold, standing unconcealed on the rim of the declivity, hands on hips, hat jauntily on the back of his head, a perfect target in the fire-light.

Two or three men, the sentry among them, prepared to use the target for the usual purpose, but stopped. The hands had suddenly moved from the hips, bringing two revolvers with them; and motion on the part of any one in front of those guns seemed distinctly inadvisable. There are three ways of covering a man, or men, with firearms; one which announces that the coverer won't fire; another that indicates he may, or may not; and still another which shrieks to the universe that he will most certainly shoot on the slightest provocation, and shoot to kill. John Arnold's method was the third.

"I asked a civil question," came the clear voice again, "and I'd like a civil reply."

"Well, who the hell are you, anyhow?" demanded the man with the bull neck.

Arnold's mouth twisted in a grin.

THE SAGE HEN

"Which name would you like?" he countered.

There was a breathless titter. It is not generally believed that bad men can giggle like schoolgirls. In point of fact, they do it much better; being, as a rule, much more nervous.

"Well, if that's the case," said the bull-necked man, "come on down. But—say. Listen."

"Yes?"

"If it ain't the case," said the bull-necked man, looking meditatively into his pannikin and pulling the lobe of his left ear, "I say, if it ain't the case—don't come down—and don't try to dodge backward, either. If you're a legal officer, just stand right still. There's a Mexican on the other side of this fire with a rifle pointin' at you."

"What's the best way down, then?"

"James," said the bull-necked man to the sentry, "bring the gent into our presence."

"I've a pony down the hillside."

"Any friends down the hillside?"

"No."

"James," said the bull-necked man, "bring the gentleman's horse into our presence as well. Shoot if necessary."

THE SAGE HEN

When the two men returned, leading the staggering mare, the leader was still standing, though the rest of the gang had seated themselves; still eating stew, though the rest had finished; and still, apparently, in the same courteous mood.

"You found the horse, I see, James," he said, ignoring John Arnold, and putting his aluminum spoon gently into his dish.

The sentry grunted.

"But why didn't you notice the gentleman's approach, eh?" asked the leader. "Eh, James?"

The sentry, warned by a subtle undertone, threw up his arm in defense; but it was too late. The bull-necked man's vast hairy fist had found its way to his jaw; and James staggered back, dropping his rifle with a clatter, to collapse as if pole-axed on the rocky floor.

The leader examined his knuckles, and picked up the spoon. He also turned his attention to Arnold.

"You wish to take up my offer of a fight for the leadership of this outfit?" he asked.

The outlaw nodded.

"May I ask how much you heard, besides that offer?"

"Everything."

The bull-necked man ate a mouthful, thoughtfully.

"Then I hope you lick me, buddy," he said, dropping the courtly manner which sat upon him like a silk waistcoat on a pig, "because if I'm still boss after we've fought it out, I'll give orders to have you shot. Get me?"

Arnold nodded again.

"All right, then," said the bull-necked man; "on those terms, have some stew."

The invitation was accepted; moreover, the newcomer, his brain working with the clear sureness of desperation, availed himself thankfully of several other things the big man handed out in addition to the pint of the communal stew.

One of these additional things was the chance to take the chill off the hearts of the watching horse lovers by insisting that his pony be fed and watered first. The other was the opportunity to issue a direct command to one of the assembly—though it was only "Fill her half-way up," and only addressed to the cook.

Had the bull-necked man relied for supremacy less on his bull neck, and more upon the gray mat-

THE SAGE HEN

ter above it, he would have watered and fed Arnold's horse with his own hands before he would have let the stranger excel him in visible consideration for the animal. And he would, had he been wise, have filled Arnold's pannikin, and fed him from a spoon, rather than allow him to assume the imperative tone. He should have been aware that, even if the newcomer won in the test of battle, the victory would be barren unless the gang had confidence in the victor's leadership; and he should have known that, from the instant any man has publicly given an order, and been obeyed, he is a boss, until proved otherwise.

Arnold was perfectly certain that he was not going to be proved otherwise.

He sat near the fire, ate slowly and sparingly, watching the blur of peering faces around him from under his eyebrows, and thinking with the refreshing ease and accuracy which had superseded the fog of exhaustion.

This was a desperate business all right—still, it was the only thing to do—it wouldn't be all settled if he knocked the leader out, either—tough lot of babies, these. That Mexican, for instance—

THE SAGE HEN

"You don't seem in any great hurry," came the voice of the bull-necked man.

"I'm not," said John Arnold deliberately and saw by various stifled grins that he had acquired another superiority over the leader in the minds of the gang —that of repartee.

He thought he would be able to make them accept him—always granting that the bull-necked man was as slow on his feet as he looked; but—would they follow him where he wanted to lead them? And if not, what would happen then? If they weren't a hundred per cent. for him, they'd be against him to the point of shooting, and he must keep alive. Joan Bruce couldn't possibly defend the Circle R with that handful of punchers; and with that mad-headed lover of hers handing the I. B. C. excuses for any kind of violence, why, it would be a massacre!

"Ready?" snapped the big man, as Arnold put down his tin dish.

"You're nervous, ain't you?" asked the diner calmly. "I was thinkin' of smoking a cigarette."

CHAPTER XI

THE human mind works strangely—with peculiar failure to see obvious things, and peculiar flashes of perspicuity when there is nothing much to be seen. The bull-necked man, who had ignored Arnold's three previous, and much greater, moral victories over him, suddenly saw that his challenger had just made a fool of him; branded him as fidgety, fight-feverish, before all his men.

As was customary with the bull-necked man at such times, a suddenly upward-sweeping curtain of vermilion-color blocked off the orange ruddy flicker of the fire. Acting as bulls and bull-necked men are apt to do when they see red—especially if the color be within their own eyes—the leader made a scrambling leap from the sitting position, and landed, with clutching hands on—the place John Arnold had just left.

For an instant, blinded by the red veil, and deafened by an internal roaring in his ears, the bull-necked man thought his enemy must be under him; and then, with a splitting ringing crash that replaced the red veil with shooting stars, followed an instant later by clear vision, something cruelly hard smashed against the side of his head.

"If you want to fight like that," said a cool voice behind him, "I can give you all you want of it."

The bull-necked man hesitated, gauging the distance of the voice from the back of his head. Having formed his estimate, he rolled over like an ungainly eel, grabbing for an ankle. The impact of a boot-toe against his mouth brought the tears to his eyes, and he scrambled to his feet cursing and spitting, to receive, while yet scarcely balanced, a terrible fist blow on the forehead.

"I know you haven't really started fighting yet," came the cool voice from an immeasurable distance. "I'm just pointing out that when you do start, you'd better start fair. You haven't got a chance, the other way. Why, I'm wanted by the police for murder with mutilation!"

"You're a liar," said the bull-necked man, dazedly feeling that this was another attempt to undermine his standing with the gang.

THE SAGE HEN

"That's the way to talk," said John Arnold. "Now come and prove it."

The bull-necked man came.

Now, in a very respectable side-street of the Chicago business district, behind the counter of a most up-to-date cigar store specializing in the box trade, the really earnest seeker can find a man who is able to tell the story of what followed much better than it can be written down; for he can illustrate the fight with titanic swings of his own horn-tattooed arms, and (if nobody else is in the store)—make vocal noises impossible to indicate in print. Everybody does not live in Chicago, however; and anyhow, this man has to confine his audience to such persons as buy brown cigarette papers and will unfeignedly believe that he was not one of the desperadoes watching the battle, but happened to be flying over the scene in an aeroplane—or—or something.

So print will have to serve.

The bull-necked man—whose name, according to what the cigar-store keeper seems to have heard in his dirigible, was Samuel Watts—hit John Arnold once under the heart, and nearly killed him outright; for it was Watts' boast, often proved, that he could stun a longhorn with one good right swing. This time, however, he failed to put all his strength behind the blow, or else there was a spirit in John Arnold out of all proportion to his weight; for, after falling and rolling feebly to escape Sam Watts' attempt to stamp on him—the challenger rose, his hands shielding the point of his jaw, and, as his assailant rushed him, shot out a bar-like left that met the point of the nose—than which there is no better mark for a man who is all but gone and wishes to gain time.

It gained him about one clear second, during which interval the watchers were astounded to hear him waste his precious reserve of breath by whispering "I promised!" According to the cigar-store man, that was all he said; and everybody was too surprised that he could speak at all, to wonder what he meant.

Besides, the bull-necked man lost no time in wiping the tears out of his eyes, and rushing again.

Arnold stopped him at arm's length with a terrible right to the cheek, blocked a right drive, stepped back from an uppercut, and from long range landed his left full in Watts' right eye. The man screamed an oath, which was cut off in the middle as his jaws were driven together by a hearty right to the chin.

Hearing the teeth clash together, Arnold, though staggering, smiled to himself. This man, though strong as a bear, was not a trained fighter, or he would not have had his mouth open. And, in view of the promise to which Arnold had alluded when the heart-punch rocked him, that was just as well. A trained fighter with brains, and a quarter of Watts' strength could, in Watts' place, have won within five minutes; and that would have been a pity, John Arnold thought; because when one man has pulled another man up from the mire, and a promise has passed between them—

He had no idea, shaken as he was, that he spoke; but according to the cigar-store man, he spoke quite clearly, while Sammy Watts was feeling for the missing tip of his tongue. John Arnold stood swaying, and remarked, in a dreamy voice:

"He picked me up, and put me on my feet again, and I promised him—"

Then Watts rushed once more. Literally insane with fury and pain, he drove in a punch to his

THE SAGE HEN

favorite target, the heart, with such force as to break through Arnold's guard and land with quite sufficient remaining velocity for any ordinary adversary. It seemed as though this, the second smashing blow on the same spot, must send Arnold to the ground, but he did not go. Defying a short-arm jab that rocked his head sickeningly to one side, he stepped forward, wrapped his long arms about Watts' head, tucked his bleeding face into Watts' neck—where stray punches might not find the jaw he was too weak to defend—and hung on. Watts' piston-like fists hammered his ribs and back; and at each hollow-sounding blow, the clinging man would groan—these are the helpless, agonized sounds which the cigar-store man can imitate so terribly. Watts pounded and hammered and roared until his own breath, though not driven by rib-snapping punches, began to roar in and out of his lungs; but still Arnold hung on.

"Finally," as the genial tobacconist puts it, "we-all got kind of sickened; and I looked away—tried to start thinkin' about somethin' else. An' the only thing I could think of was that this stranger'd gasped out about somebody havin' picked him outa the mud, an' all that. Well, bein' in Hurst County, the words kind of connected up with somethin' I'd seen in the newspapers, after—er—I'd gone on that trip to Mexico that time. An' I just got an inspiration—that this guy was the one old Man Bruce's son'd picked up from bein' a criminal. I didn't get no further than that—then."

His meditations were interrupted, first, by the sudden cessation of the horrid groans, as Sam Watts, exhausted, dropped his fists to his sides; and then by something still more sensational.

For suddenly, John Arnold loosed his grip of Watts' neck, stepped back, and shot forward a last punch containing every ounce of the strength accumulated during that dearly-purchased clinch. It was no fancy blow; a simple left to the jaw—but backed by everything John Arnold owned, both physically and nervously; and it landed.

Sammy Watts crumpled at the knees, shot over backward, and lay perfectly still.

They expected Arnold, his work done, to fall also, but he didn't. He stood bolt upright and motionless, as if a movement would upset his balance; and in a weak, yet masterful voice, he called for a

THE SAGE HEN

rifle. The cigar-store man—apparently reaching down from his aeroplane for the purpose—handed him one. It was a B. S. A. sporter—.303 British, with a bolt action; and it was some time before the dazed man who held it realized that it was not his own lever-worked Winchester. Finally, he found the bolt-handle, opened it, glanced at the gleam of brass and cupronickel in the magazine, and slammed the rifle shut and loaded.

"Am I boss now?" he asked.

There came an awed murmur of assent.

"Then listen," came the faint determined tones. "Plans are all changed. . . . Wait a minute. . . . I said plans were all changed, didn't I? Well, so they are. If I'm boss, this outfit isn't going on any plundering expedition, while the I. B. C.'s busy—busy—wait a minute. Busy plundering an orphan girl, an'—while—the sheriff of the county's—busy helpin' 'em. We're going to fight for Joan Bruce."

There was a silence.

"He's crazy," said some one in a whisper.

But Arnold caught it.

"Crazy?" he cried, his voice suddenly stronger.

THE SAGE HEN

"You fools. I'm not crazy! I know you better than you know yourselves. It's you that are crazy. You're a bunch of scared thugs and what-not that've been hiding in Mexico until you don't know yourselves from yellow dogs. You think all you want is plunder and booze; but you don't. What you want is a chance to come back—and you're ashamed to ask for it. I'm handing it to you on a silver platter, with my blood on it, and you say I'm crazy! You know better!"

Somebody in the back of the gang got to his feet. It was the Mexican cook.

"I don't," he said.

"Then you can get out," said John Arnold. "And all like you. You *are* yellow dogs."

"I—"

"Look out you're not dead yellow dogs!"

There was a silence; the dying fire crackled.

"All the same," said a reflective voice, "what do we get out of it, buddy?"

"Jobs—Circle R," gasped Arnold, "if we win. Death—if we lose. Anyhow—self-respect."

"Self-respect?" asked a voice.

"Crazy!" whispered the man who had whispered before.

THE SAGE HEN

There was a long pause, during which John Arnold felt his way blindly to a flat rock, and sat heavily down on it, rifle still ready.

"Oh, I dunno," said the man who now keeps the cigar store in Chicago. "I'd kind of like to look myself in the face again."

There was another long pause.

"Let's sleep on it," said another voice slowly.

"Go ahead," said the man with the rifle. "I'm sentry."

And in spite of protests, and the apparent absurdity of the attempt, the new leader sat there until dawn was in the sky; a sentry over his hard-won command—and a sort of armed image; whose tall figure and the gleam of whose rifle-barrel they saw whenever they looked around during their conferences. For they did not sleep on the question; instead, rolled in their blankets, they talked all night, in low tones. All except the Mexican cook and two other men. They slept peacefully and heavily, —like dogs, and Sam Watts, who was still unconscious.

It was after three o'clock when one of the gang approached John Arnold and told him roughly that he'd better quit this foolishness and sleep.

THE SAGE HEN

"Decided yet?" asked the man with the rifle. "I don't sleep—except among my own men."

The delegate hesitated.

"You're fixin' to fight for this skirt because her brother picked you up an'— You're that guy, ain't you?"

Arnold stood up.

"Yes," he said curtly.

Through the dim gray light of the dawn, the rest of the gang moved up to listen.

"You promised him—somep'n? Or you're grateful to him, or somep'n?"

"Yes. But for you men, the proposition's—"

"All right. We're satisfied about that. But—"

"But what?"

There was a steely edge to the voice that stopped the delegate with his mouth open.

"But what?"

The man who now keeps the cigar store in Chicago stepped forward.

"I've been tellin' 'em," he said bluntly, "that though you're seemingly full of gratitude to young Bruce now, I read in the paper that you—murdered him."

THE SAGE HEN

It was rather a chilly early morning up there in the hills. As John Arnold raised his eyes, everybody in that dim, gray, ghostly gathering shivered more or less.

"Well?" he asked.

There was a long silence.

"Well," asked the first delegate with difficulty, "is—is it true?"

"The—sheriff—of Hurst County—is after me now—on that charge."

The sun sent a beam over the edge of the depression.

"Yeah," said one man, "but suppose he catches you—how'll you plead, prisoner at the bar—guilty, or not guilty?"

Arnold drew a long breath; and at the same moment, the wandering sunbeam found his face.

"Guilty!" he said.

The man who had asked the question drew a long breath, too; he was the oldest man present, and his eyes were fixed on Arnold's lighted face.

"Well," he said, after full consideration, "anyhow, I guess I'll ride with you. But I dunno why."

All of them, in fact—except the Mexican, and the

other two men, and Sammy Watts when he regained consciousness—guessed they would ride with John Arnold, and they none of them knew why.

They tried to dope it out, in solemn conclave, all the afternoon, while Arnold slept, but they were no nearer a solution when, as the evening shadows began to lengthen, they mounted and, with their new leader at their head, rode down toward the disputed plains through the dusk.

CHAPTER XII

WORD was flying around Hurst County—word from the thin lips of Mr. William Rigby himself—and Hurst County was stirring as the night crept down. The word was to the effect that a grand massed attack would be made on the Circle R ranch at midnight; and, quite naturally, the stirring of the county consisted of stretches for gun belts, and the running of thumb-nails across the yellow-paper wrappings of cartridge boxes. Also, there arose from the armed ranch houses surrounding the Circle R, certain discontented murmurings, as ex-punchers from various parts of the country, now gunmen for the I. B. C., grumbled that this wasn't what they had signed on for. The idea had been a summer's free keep, sprinkled with skirmishes; not one big and immediate push, after which their services would be no longer required.

It was difficult to murmur in Hurst County without being heard by Mr. William Rigby.

THE SAGE HEN

This particular susurrus reached him within an hour after he had issued the mobilization order; and he received it blandly, sitting in his room at the Hurst Seat Hotel, sipping caffeinless coffee, as was his wont, and reading the syndicated humor of the *Longhorn City Democrat*. It was the sheriff who brought the news. Mr. Rigby received him with the courteous respect he always showed for the law and its representatives so long as they were in his pay.

"Well?" he inquired gently, marking his place in the humorous column with his long and grisly thumb.

"Well, Mr. Rigby," said the sheriff, "the boys are kickin'. I dunno but that's all I got to say. They're kickin' because they weren't figurin' on all this rough stuff right away, an'—"

"But they'll obey orders, won't they?" asked the viceroy of Hurst County.

"Well, yes—"

"Then suppose we let them kick?" smiled Mr. Rigby. "Good exercise. Good evening."

The sheriff did not move.

"Well?" asked Mr. Rigby again. "Something else?"

"Well, of course it's no business of mine to advise you—"

"Quite so," said Mr. Rigby. The light from the oil lamp above his head could scarcely have been too strong for any one, so poor was the quality of the oil and so dirty was its chimney; but the gentleman with the newspaper turned away from it nevertheless, and shaded his brows with his hand. Instantly, he changed from a rather hungry-looking little lawyer into a sinister figure with a pool of shadow where eyes should have been.

"What, then," came the gentle voice, "is this advice you have no business to give, Mr. Sheriff?"

"About this attack to-night."

"Yes. Go on."

The sheriff perspired freely and played with the brim of his hat.

"Well, sir," he said, staring at his boot-toes, "it's like this. A lot of the boys don't feel easy in their minds about it. What I mean, they're grumbling, and— Well, sir, you see, it's kind of unexpected, and so sudden, an' all; they haven't kind of got used to the situation yet—I mean, just goin' out cold and attackin' this ranch, 'specially since it's a skirt that's running it—"

"Rubbish," said Mr. Rigby without moving. "Rubbish! Anything else?"

The sheriff writhed.

"Well, sir, there's other things, too. I mean, for instance, there's this jasper Arnold at large, an' on the girl's side. They're kind of leery of him. He's got a bad reputation, seems. Some of the boys heard of him in Mexico."

"It's your fault he's at large," said Rigby. "Anyhow—one man against three hundred or so—Rubbish! Anything besides that?"

"This is kind of rough business we're gonna do to-night, Mr. Rigby," said the sheriff. "And I'm—they're more or less wondering what's goin' to happen about old Bill Garfield, over there in Three Pines County. I—they think he's just as likely as not to come over here and raise hell in the name of the law, an'—"

"No legal standing here. Seventy-odd years old. Rubbish! What else?"

The sheriff stared into the pool of darkness under the long thin hand, and weakened at the knees.

"Oh, nothing else, I guess," he stammered. "I—"

"What else?" snarled the gentle voice suddenly.

"Well—well, Mr. Rigby—well, one or two of the boys that was in that fight at the Circle R last night are sayin' they got a barb-wire entanglement an' everythin', an' they're desperate, the skirt an' the men she's got with her—an' there's folks goin' to be killed if we make this here rush, an' they're wonderin' why. I mean, what we were goin' to do was surround the Circle R, an' cut their fences, an' drive their cattle off, an' not let 'em get any food or supplies, an' starve 'em out, so I understood, an' no fightin' except when they tried to break through, or the like of that."

Slowly, the viceroy removed his shading hand from his eyes, nodded; and with equal deliberation drew forth his watch. It was exactly eight o'clock. Methodically, he gave the stem half a dozen winding turns before putting it back in his pocket.

"Nevertheless, they will attack?" he asked thoughtfully.

"Oh, yeah. They don't like this idea of layin' hands on the girl, even if she ain't to be hurt, but— they'll do it all right."

"And why?" asked Rigby, smiling.

The sheriff wriggled with mental effort.

THE SAGE HEN

"I guess," he said at last, "that they're afraid not to, Mr. Rigby."

The viceroy chuckled.

"I guess so too, Sheriff," he remarked. "And in that case, explanations as to why we're attacking and all that kind of thing, are rather superfluous, don't you think?"

"Y—y—yes, sir."

"Nevertheless," said Mr. Rigby, "as soon as you leave this room, you will send one member of your posse—I suppose they're down-stairs?—on a round of the ranches to give out the news that Mr. David Grant is our prisoner, and to remind all whom it may concern that the other dangerous criminal, John Arnold, is in hiding, and out of the fight."

"Yessir—"

"Don't go. One moment. And in return for your very interesting news, I'm going to give you, Mr. Sheriff, a special job. There'll be no extra pay, but the honor, I'm sure, will compensate. If our men are nervous and unwilling, they may get careless. You will attend to the capture of Miss Joan Bruce—unhurt—and her delivery to me personally, here in Hurst Seat. You see?"

The sheriff drew a long breath.

"I'll explain to you," said Mr. Rigby, "that the—er—arrest of that young lady, personally, is the reason for this attack to-night. She, personally, is the reason why our plan of blockading the Circle R until the owner would sell for a—er—reasonable figure, has failed. She, personally, is the owner; and she gave me the impression that no amount of blockading, starvation, or cattle-driving would induce her to sell under a figure which may have represented the value of the ranch before it became so—er—run down, but which now—well—we needn't go into that. Suffice it to say that the only thing to be done is to argue with her personally. This attack to-night is for the purpose of bringing her where I can argue—conveniently. You will see that the attack does not fail of this purpose."

The sheriff licked his lips. He also looked around the room, very much in the manner of a trapped animal seeking an avenue of escape. He was in full possession of the details of two attempts to kidnap Joan Bruce; and the prospect of a third, in which those details might be repeated with himself for the victim, was far from pleasing. He was cursed with something in the nature of an imagination; which, at this moment, was presenting to him a sort of mental movie dealing with one scene only: an indefinite background which was the Circle R, a desperate fight raging, with Joan Bruce for its center, and himself standing by, bound to bid the attackers spare no effort to win, but also bound to protect Joan Bruce from stray bullets, and all the chances of close fighting.

"You see?" asked Mr. Rigby, smiling.

"It—don't—seem possible," said the sheriff.

"It had better," said Mr. Rigby, continuing to smile.

He turned away, and picked up his newspaper.

"If I might advise, further," he observed, looking up and down the column in search of his place, "I would not, if I were you, try to make it seem more possible by getting drunk, because if you are drunk, you won't be yourself, and if you are not yourself, Mr. Sheriff, you may fail to deliver Miss Bruce to me; and if you fail to deliver Miss Bruce to me, you will assuredly go to jail for at least fifteen—"

Mr. Rigby had found his place, and was interested.

On the ominous numeral, his voice tailed off absently, and, as he read, his thin lips were revisited by the blissful smile of the simple-minded and innocent.

The sheriff, staring at this spectacle, dry-lipped, for perhaps thirty seconds, turned, opened the door softly; and, as if walking in awe of something, passed slowly out of the room.

The night, in whose shadow he rejoined his waiting posse, was now dark-blue, and full of the Rio Grande mists by which a blind man could tell dark from daylight.

"What happened?" asked one of the men.

The sheriff stared at him dazedly.

"Nothin'," he whispered. "I mean—nothin'. What did you think'd happen, you fool?"

His voice grew stronger as he used it, but the dazed expression continued to mask the usual bold viciousness of his eyes.

"I want," he said, looking around the circle of his supporters, "somebody to carry a message—go 'round the ranch houses again."

There was a unanimous groan, but he disregarded it. There was Lefty Jeeks—no, Lefty was reliable, and when it came to that final fight at the Circle R, he'd want Lefty Jeeks right by him; he felt a warm affection for Lefty Jeeks; and for Ham-bone Parsons, and for Tex Walty, with his knife—all dear useful friends for a man in trouble.

However, that guy with the white eyelashes wouldn't be much use.

"Hey, you," said the sheriff. "You'll do. Get a fresh horse an' go tell everybody that that guy Dave Grant's in the lock-up, where he can't do no harm. An' there's a bonus for everybody that's out to-night."

"Everybody?" asked the man with white eyelashes wearily.

"Yeah, everybody!" snarled the sheriff. "An' you can add this—"

He thought.

"You can tell 'em," he went on, "that this Sage Hen's got to be arrested alive, an' unhurt, an' that anybody who don't do his part to arrestin' her, or hurts her while he's doin' it, 'll have me to answer to. Get that?"

"Y-yes," said the messenger.

"Who do you answer to?" asked Lefty Jeeks;

THE SAGE HEN

but the sheriff, fresh from being crushed under the silky weight of Mr. Rigby, was too busy regaining a feeling of superiority by bullying White Eyelashes, to hear uncomfortable questions.

White Eyelashes was really an easy person to bully—almost too easy.

For instance, when, half an hour later, he rode bang into the middle of a band of horsemen commanded by John Arnold, he was very easily bullied into telling them everything he knew—all about the projected attack, all about the kidnapping which was its projected result, all about the forces to be employed, and so forth. Having given all the information of which he stood possessed, he apparently raised no serious objection even to being knocked out, and left unconscious on the prairie, his face absolutely blocking one exit of a prairie-dog hole, his arms and legs spread about untidily among the growing grass.

Aside from being cowardly and extremely stupid, White Eyelashes was really quite an admirable character, diligent, faithful and conscientious. When he recovered his wits half an hour later, the first thing he did was to deduce the direction taken by

THE SAGE HEN

his assailants, from the trail visible in the dewy and moonlit grass. Having decided it made a bee-line for the Circle R, the second-thing he did was to recapture his pony, mount, and, despite a splitting headache, ride belly-to-earth toward Hurst Seat with the news.

It was his cowardice that, before he reached Five Mile, made him pull his nag to a halt, and quake at the thought of the reception he would get from the sheriff of Hurst County.

It was his conscientiousness which made him consider that, if through his fault, reinforcements had gone to join this Sage Hen his boss was after, it was up to him, White Eyelashes, to make some kind of amends.

It was his stupidity that made him decide that, since he dared not face his boss and warn him, the next best thing to do would be to provide compensating reinforcements for the sheriff's party.

What made him determine—as he did determine—that the best way to get these reinforcements was to ride for Three Pines, and tell the whole story to old Bill Garfield, it is difficult to say.

Probably that crack on the head.

CHAPTER XIII

IT WAS a still clear night, with the moon riding high; the sky a misty fawn color backed with an elusive blue, and the far stretching prairies gray-blue and mysterious. Perfect silence seemed to fill the space between earth and sky, a silence rather intensified than broken by the pud-pud-pud of John Arnold's cavalcade as it cantered across the short grass, by the creak of leather from the saddles and cinches, and the occasional snort of a horse. With unknown things ahead, it was a silence rather trying to the nerves; and, a mile from the Circle R, one of the men broke it.

"Hey, boss," he called. "Don't we get any orders for this trip?"

There was no answer for perhaps another twenty-five yards, and then Arnold spoke in a peculiar voice—almost as if he were asleep in the saddle. Another peculiar thing might have been noticed, had any one present been in a frame of mind to pay at-

THE SAGE HEN

tention to details. The leader was holding his treasured Winchester as no man in his right mind has carried a rifle since the days of archery; across the horn of the saddle, muzzle pointing to the right, the butt away from out of reach to the left, and he was holding it in this position with the palms of his hands, which also clutched the bridle in a clumsy pawing grasp—as if he had lost the use of his fingers.

"What you say?" he asked. "Orders?"

"Yeah," said another man. "Orders, mister. We don't know what we're goin' to do. You ain't figurin' to stand us up in the way of this here young army the I. B. C.'s sendin', are you?"

"Army?" said Arnold hazily.

He pulled his pony to a stop, and turned around in his saddle. The company behind him gathered in a dim semicircle, obviously ill-at-ease and doubtful; and, for a moment, Arnold, in a fog of utter fatigue, doubted his own ability to make them follow him any farther. In point of fact, his command hung by a hair. He had brought these men down from the hills by force of personality and the promise that they were to engage in the rather piquant pastime of guerrilla warfare. Now, choked by weariness, his personality was not a factor in the case, while the pleasant vista of shooting and riding away had been replaced in the minds of those present by a most unattractive picture of themselves, standing shoulder to shoulder with a bunch of perfect strangers, and being annihilated by enormously superior numbers.

"Yeah," said the man who had first spoken. "We like you right well, mister, but if your idea is to stand us up to be shot down again, why, I think I'll be joggin' home again, if it's all the same to you. An' I don't see why it shouldn't be the same to you, because us tryin' to stand off two-three hundred bad men, an' gettin' killed doin' it, ain't goin' to do anybody any good."

"No," said Arnold.

Desperately, he was trying to make his brain work; and it was refusing to respond to his call. He realized, as he sat staring at the waiting desperadoes, that any attempt to outfight the I. B. C. with such a pitifully small force was useless and suicidal; surely he must have had some better idea than that; yet digging painfully through the jumbled contents of his tired mind, retracing his thoughts back to the interview with White Eyelashes, the haggard-eyed leader could find nothing of use.

His command, staring at him, fidgeted under his vacant gaze.

"Wait a minute," he said slowly, looking away from them.

"Listen," he said, a moment later.

His eyes had fastened, independently of any desire on his part, upon the outline of a little grove of trees near at hand; rather a peculiar outline against the sky; it seemed to suggest something to him, as he mulled drearily over the facts that the I. B. C. was planning to swoop down in its might and both occupy the Circle R and kidnap its owner at one fell blow. The occupation of the ranch would be of little importance; the kidnapping of Joan, the application of tortures, perhaps, to make her complete the legal forms of selling the ranch at the I. B. C. price, was—

"What are we supposed to be listening to?" asked a voice from the shadowy semicircle.

"This," said John Arnold.

THE SAGE HEN

And, speaking in a clear voice which seemed to him to be quite independent of his own volition, he explained the plan, which, almost without his knowledge, had crept into his exhausted mind.

"This is the idea," he told the men. "This attack's an attempt to get hold of Miss Bruce in person. They've tried to capture her before, but—but they've failed. This time they won't fail; they'll take her prisoner and make her sell the ranch, or they'll kill her, and get it for a song that way. Probably kill her; for she'll fight to the last cartridge—that is, if she's still at the Circle R when the I. B. C. men get there."

"You mean—we'll tell her they're coming, an' she'll git out?"

"No," said John Arnold. "She won't get out—especially for me."

"Knows about—you—an' her brother?" asked the elderly man of the gang.

"Yes."

There was a silence.

"Well then, what are we goin' to do?"

Arnold drew a long breath.

"Kidnap her ourselves."

There was another silence.

"Well?" snarled Arnold suddenly, "yes or no? Are you with me, or aren't you? If you're not, say so; and I'll go ahead myself. If you're coming, come along. We've no time to lose. But if you're not—don't let anybody hint that maybe I'm not on the square in this. For if anybody does, by the living God, I'll kill him!"

"All right, buddy," said the elderly ruffian soothingly. He chuckled. "Me, I think it's a fine idea. By gosh, fancy gettin' that army out, an' then findin' nobody home to fight it!"

A companion chuckle ran around the gang.

"Hadn't we better be movin', then?" asked the proud possessor of a wrist-watch—he was also the man who owned the B. S. A. sporting rifle, and he had collected both novelties from an English tourist in Mexico; by what means, it were perhaps as well not to inquire. "We've only got an hour."

Within fifteen minutes, they were in sight of the Circle R's barbed-wire fences, and, simultaneously, the targets for a .45-70 Springfield bullet which, leaving the barricade with a dull boom and flash of black powder, droned five feet overhead.

THE SAGE HEN

"Hey!" said the man with the wrist-watch, as if a new thought had just occurred to him—as indeed it had. "We can't shoot back!"

Arnold licked his lips.

"An' they're goin' to plug us, just the same's they would the I. B. C.! Hey, wow! That's no fun!"

The Springfield roared again, with equal lack of effect. Moonlight is bad illumination for old-fashioned Buffington sights, especially when the eye behind them is half-closed, as Sloan's was, from lack of sleep combined with nervous exhaustion. Furthermore, the big man had gained, through continual firing, a childish terror of the concussion and recoil of the heavy rifle. As he pulled the trigger, he flinched like a novice, and groaned pitifully as the steel-shod butt hammered his shoulder. Of course his shots went high.

"Nobody's going to get hurt," said John Arnold. "Listen. Half of you cut around to the rear—see? I put up—I mean, I told 'em to put up—that barbed wire; and there's a place near the barn where they only used four-foot stakes. It's new wire, an' there's moon enough for the horses to see it. You can jump that and be in among them while their

171

attention's out here. Now, you club your guns, for the man that shoots, I'll kill!"

"They ain't goin' to keep their attention out here," said the eldest man.

"They are."

"Why?"

"Because I'm going to ride forward and talk to them, and they'll see—most of you—sitting your horses back here. Six'll be enough to cut around back. You six!"

His finger indicated half a dozen men who chanced to be bunched together.

"You know what to do? You club your guns, and don't hurt anybody you don't have to."

"Yes, but—"

"But what?"

"If you're gonna ride forward an' talk to 'em—"

"Yes?"

"Well, do they know about—you—an' the lady's brother?"

"Yes. That's what'll keep their attention on me."

"Why, they're liable to shoot you on sight!"

"They're liable to try. It's your job to stop 'em before they've tried too much."

THE SAGE HEN

"Well—" said one of the half-dozen, partly hesitant, partly in admiration. Admiration won. Ordinary human pride would not permit six men to hesitate about a flank attack, while one man was already riding forward to protect them by offering himself as a cockshot. The flanking party, after watching Arnold trot forward perhaps ten yards, looked at one another, clucked to their ponies, and moved away into the night. They paused once, hearing again the bellow of the Springfield, and the crack of two more modern rifles from the barricade; but immediately afterward they heard the voice of Arnold raised in a shout of "Hi! Don't shoot!" and an answering yell, "Who are you?" and avoiding stony ground with its attendant noise, they pushed on again.

"If he answers that," said one of the flankers to another, "they'll plug him first thing."

And he did not answer it—because he had no need to. Joan Bruce, on the porch of the ranch house with a pair of field-glasses to her eyes, had recognized him even before Sloan shouted the question.

"It's John Arnold," she cried, in a strange,

hoarse voice, and then, instantly: "Don't shoot, Sloan!"

The big man turned his head and snarled over the butt of his rifle.

"Don't shoot? Why not shoot? You want me to kiss him?"

The other men at the wire fence, exhausted as Sloan, stared apathetically at their woman boss.

"He may have something to say," said the Sage Hen. "You can—shoot him later—if he needs it."

"Hi!" came the hail from out on the prairie. "Hi! Don't shoot!"

The tall figure on the horse was about a hundred and fifty yards away, and in silhouette against the moonlit mist. Sloan grinned and fingered his trigger.

"All right! But stop there!" he roared. And to the man on the right, in a low tone. "Fetch Dick and Pinky from the back fence. I can't hold straight no more. We'll give him a volley."

"What you got to say, Arnold?" he yelled again.

There was a pause; the silhouetted horseman had reined in and stopped. Now he played for time.

"Oh, you know me already, do you?" he asked.

THE SAGE HEN

Sloan laughed.

"You bet! An' we know your range, too!"

"Then I don't suppose," shouted Arnold, "that you'll believe anything I have to say, will say?"

Sloan gave a mocking roar.

"I didn't think you would," came the distant comment. "But I'll tell you all the same. Are you listening?"

"Yes, you skunk, an' we're cocking our guns, too!" It was in a low voice; and Sloan added: "Pinky, you take his horse—you too, Dick. The rest of us can fix him personally. Then I guess that bunch behind him'll charge us, but—"

"Are you listening?"

"Yes!" bellowed Sloan. "What is it?"

"I'm here to tell you," called John Arnold, "that three-quarters of an hour from now, three hundred men—I. B. C. men—are going to attack you and kidnap Miss Bruce. David Grant is arrested and locked up in Hurst Seat jail; and this kidnapping's going to be under color of arresting Miss Bruce and you-all for firing on some Lazy F men who claim to have been passing the Circle R last night."

There was a snigger along the fence.

THE SAGE HEN

"Passing is good," said Dick dreamily.

"Are you still listening?"

"Listening and laughing," shouted Pinky Pawson. "Tell us some more, Mister Murderer."

There was a considerable pause.

"Well, I'm here to help you, if you want my help," said Arnold, "or if you don't, for that matter."

Sloan, whose slow brain had failed to extract anything but rage out of Arnold's appearance, or anything but puzzlement out of his earlier remarks, understood this, all right—or thought he did. It was an attempt by this double-crossing International Beef Concern thug, this murderer, to gain their confidence again, and thus save his employers even the slight loss of life attendant upon taking the Circle R by storm. Also, the proposal was an insult to the intelligence. Suddenly, the blood drummed in Mr. Sloan's ears. He wanted to say something adequate to his feelings in the matter; but his slow-moving words seemed to stick and mushroom out somewhere under his heart. There was nothing he could do in fact, but throw up his rifle and fire, with an oath as the hammer fell.

THE SAGE HEN

Before Dick and Corliss and Pinky Dawson could follow suit, two things happened. John Arnold swayed in his saddle and, without even a clutch for the horn, fell to the ground.

And, simultaneously, with a yell and a thud, and a heavy rolling clatter as one of the horses tripped on the top barbed wire—the flanking party jumped the fence and charged into the middle of the enclosure.

It was not much of an affair—considered as a fight; it was a poor sequel to the valiant resistance made by this same garrison to much superior forces, the night before. Sloan, fumbling sleepily and furiously with the hammer and hinged breech of his demicannon, was punched cleanly on the point of the jaw, and sent to bask peacefully in a Milky Way of stars. Corliss, Dick and Pinky Pawson, struggling to arise from the prone positions they had assumed for the sake of steadiness in their shooting at Arnold, were flattened to the earth, disarmed and then allowed to rise, under the superintendance of the man with the B. S. A. rifle. The only fight worthy of the name was put up by a wiry little man named Williams—the ranch cook; who knocked one of the flanking party out with a revolver barrel, and would have shot another at a range of two feet, had not the palm of his hand, perspiring with excitement, slipped off the hammer of the gun he was trying to fan.

Even Joan Bruce, really the deadliest of the defenders, was captured with comparative ease. Forty-eight hours' vigilance had taken the edge off her alertness, and there was a delay of perhaps five seconds while she stared at the invaders wide-eyed, forgetful of the automatic pistol that hung at her belt. By the time her hand had found the butt, a giant of Arnold's command had spied her in the gloom of the porch, and as she drew and leveled the gun he rushed toward her, shouting something unintelligible about not shooting, and all this being for her own good. As she fired four shots at him, Joan reflected dully that nobody seemed to care to be shot, this evening.

Then the pistol was snatched out of her hand and flung far out of sight.

"You don't want to do that, miss," protested a hoarse heavy voice. "We're takin' you away so's the I. B. C. can't get you, an'—"

THE SAGE HEN

The voice went on, but the Sage Hen did not hear it. She had, in fact, sagged forward against the possessor of the heavy voice, and fainted.

It was exactly twenty minutes to twelve, and the columns of I. B. C. attackers were converging rapidly on their objective, when Arnold's men, with their leader across his horse, and Joan Bruce lying limply in the arms of the elderly man, left the Circle R with its disarmed garrison, and scurried away like moon-cast shadows, toward the hills.

CHAPTER XIV

IT WAS in the brick-paved, oil-lit corridor of the Hurst Seat jail, whither he had gone to taunt David Grant with what he supposed to be transpiring at the Circle R, that Mr. William Rigby received news of what actually had occurred. The news was conveyed to him by Mr. William Garfield, sheriff of Three Pines County—and, since the Hurst County peace officer had apparently run away into Mexico—by self-appointment, sheriff of Hurst County as well.

"I asked him to stay," remarked Mr. Garfield argumentatively; "but he didn't seem to think you'd be pleased with him, Mr. Rigby—though why a peace officer should worry about what a civilian like you's pleased with or not pleased with, I dunno. Anyhow, he would not be prevented from skedaddling, nor would this bunch of thugs which don't appear to be hired by anybody, or to have any respect for anybody or anything, be persuaded to get off the Circle R land; but I will attend to them to-morrow."

"No—legal—standing," said Mr. Rigby, who seemed to be having great difficulty with his breathing—and with his heart action as well, if his alarming pallor were any indication.

"No," said Mr. Garfield casually. "I suppose I haven't. But in the meantime, the dope is that this Arnold has kidnapped the girl and scooted for the hills."

"You must—get him—at once," whispered Rigby. "Sheriff—thousand dollars reward—ten thousand—"

Mr. Garfield scratched his gray side-whiskers thoughtfully.

"A person would almost think," he observed with an engaging smile, "that this Arnold had kidnapped somebody you wanted to kidnap yourself, however absurd such an idea might seem."

"He's a murderer!" cried Rigby. "It's your duty to arrest—"

"Thought you said I had no legal standing?" said Mr. Garfield. "Ah, well. We'll see. Rum-ti-tum! Who's this in the jail? Not Mr. David Grant?"

Rigby, trembling all over, and with a strangely twitching mouth, was leaning back against the wall of the jail corridor.

"Then—you won't go after Arnold?" he said. "You won't get after this—murderer and kidnapper?"

"We'll see," said the aged sheriff encouragingly. "We'll see! Meantime, I asked you if this is young Dave Grant in this cell—though I see it actually is—and what's he here for?"

"He's awaiting trial on a charge of disorderly conduct, Bill," said the turnkey.

Mr. Garfield looked from the turnkey to Mr. Rigby, and scratched his whiskers some more.

"Well, that's a good conservative charge," he said. "I'll look into the right and wrongs of it tomorrow. What's that?"

He was addressing David Grant. The young man, unshaven, extremely pale, and apparently unable to speak above a hoarse whisper, was half leaning against, half hanging on, the steel-barred door of his cell.

"Let me out," he was saying. "Bill Garfield, let me out!"

THE SAGE HEN

Mr. Garfield wagged his finger roguishly.

"That's what they all say," he observed.

"For God's sake, let me out before I go mad!" cried the boy, his voice suddenly rising to a wild shout. "I want to kill him! I want to take him by the throat and strangle him to death! He said to trust him—he'd killed her brother, and now, this— Let me out, for God's sake!"

Mr. Garfield looked at him and shook his head.

"I do believe," he said, in his usual soft gentle voice, "that if you was let out, you'd go and interfere with the processes of the law, as made and provided in such cases. Surely you realize that all this sort of thing's up to me? Well, then!"

The old gentleman put on his hat.

"Then—you're going after Arnold?" asked Rigby.

"I will see about it, Mr. Civilian, I will see," said old Bill Garfield; and left the jail.

Looking like his own shadow in the dim oil light, Mr. William Rigby stepped over to the door of David Grant's cell. His face was white and working, his hands still trembled, but he had regained control of his voice and, apparently, of his wits.

THE SAGE HEN

"You hear that?" he asked his prisoner, smiling. "You hear what your dear friend, the sheriff, says? He says he'll see about it—when this man who murdered Joan Bruce's brother has got the girl up there in the hills—alone!"

"Let me out!" gasped Grant, shaking the door. "Let me out, for God's sake!"

It had, apparently, been Mr. Rigby's intention to goad, taunt and mock his prisoner, but now a new idea seemed to occur to him.

"What would you do, for instance, if you were out?" he inquired.

"I'd kill him!" shouted the man behind the bars. "I'd dog him to the ends of the earth, and kill him with my bare hands. I'll hound him barefoot into hell, but I'll kill him. I'll kill him! For God's sake, let me out. Give me a horse and let me go."

Mr. William Rigby was shocked to the core of his being.

"After threats like that?" he said, though he was unable to keep just a suspicion of tremor out of his voice. "On the contrary! You'll stay in there until this person you want to murder is safe in the custody of the law—if he ever is in the custody of the law."

THE SAGE HEN

"Let me out!" groaned Grant. "Let me out to kill him!"

Smiling and shaking his head, Mr. Rigby strolled away, down the corridor toward the door.

"You're a very dangerous man," he protested pleasantly.

But at the door, he gripped the turnkey who followed him by the wrist, until his bony fingers bruised that official's arm, turned a face which, in its damp pallor and in point of expression resembled nothing so much as a devil-mask, and in a whisper like the hiss of a snake, uttered an order in three words:

"Let him out!"

CHAPTER XV

SIX days elapsed; and on the evening of the seventh, the ranch house and barns of the Circle R burned to the ground with a glare distinctly visible from that pocket in the Hurst County hills where John Arnold lay under a shelter of branches, very ill; and where Joan Bruce was fighting with white-faced steady fury against her gentle, courteous, yet firm captivity among John Arnold's men.

It is so easy to say a day, or six days, or a year "elapsed." Pleasant, too. In addition to saving the trouble of cataloguing all sorts of things, it endows one with the comfortable but misleading idea that a day can consist of nothing more than one revolution of the earth around the sun; whereas, for the purposes of humanity, it consists, essentially, less of a certain number of hours, than of a certain number of deeds. And whatever may be the case with Time, the philosophers of all ages agree that no deed can ever be said to "elapse"—that is, to finish, cease and determine, and pass into the past. Big or small, good or bad, a deed once performed exerts its effect, good or bad, big or small, upon humanity to the end of time.

To describe every deed, even of one man, for one whole day, is beyond the power of any pen; and the six days following the kidnapping of Joan Bruce were filled with violent action on the part of five hundred men in Hurst County; mostly I. B. C. men, combing the countryside, especially the hills, for Arnold and his gang—and particularly—for Joan Bruce.

For two days—until old Bill Garfield could surround himself with a posse of his own men, imported from Three Pines County, and headed by Mr. Garfield's rawboned deputy, Jake Henson—a large party of I. B. C. men stayed out of the search, occupying the Circle R ranch, and trying to assist its absent owner by rounding up what few cattle remained—so clumsily, however, that every single animal escaped, to be no more seen.

On the third day, these gentlemen were set free from this arduous work by Mr. William Garfield in person, who rode up, followed by a jingling and extremely ugly-looking party of Three Pines men

THE SAGE HEN

and went so far as to say that he'd blow the brains out of the man who was on Circle R land within five minutes from the time he stopped talking.

To make sure his ideas on this subject should be regarded with proper respect, Mr. Garfield even left a guard of his own men in possession of the ranch; but on the fourth day, this force was withdrawn. The aged sheriff, who, in spite of his casual remarks to Mr. Rigby, had been after John Arnold tooth and nail ever since he took over the responsibility for the law in Hurst County, was finding the Hurst County hills more complicated, or John Arnold's gang more mobile and cunning than he had expected; and, with perspiration beading his wrinkled cheeks every time he thought of the plight of Joan Bruce, he was throwing every last man he controlled into the hunt. He had on his hands the rather unpleasant problems not only of arresting John Arnold for murder and abduction, and of rescuing Joan Bruce from captivity; but also of rescuing John Arnold from illegal death at the hands of David Grant, and of seeing that Joan Bruce was not "rescued" into still more dangerous captivity, by the International Beef Concern's searchers.

THE SAGE HEN

"It's them that's prevented me from gettin' him, Jake," Mr. Garfield said through the few teeth age had left him, as he rode homeward with his deputy, on the fifth day, after a fruitless ten hours in the hills.

"I don't see—" said Mr. Henson.

"You don't see, you dumb jug, you!" snarled his venerable chief. "What you see and don't see! My God! Can't you see this Rigby guy's blocking us at every turn? You think he wants Joan Bruce recovered—by us? No! He wants to kidnap her on his own account; and none of his men has the brains to do it. Do you think he really wants Arnold arrested and legally tried? No! He wants him killed before he can open his trap."

"You told me," said Mr. Henson painstakingly, "that Rigby kinda got on your nerves, orderin' you to go get the jasper."

"To go get him—yes," said Mr. Garfield, "and to bring him where he could be lynched, see? Now Mr. Rigby's kinda got to know me better, he ain't so keen on me exercisin' my office. That's why you an' me an' our little posse can't start out anywhere without fifty strangers joinin' us—an' makin' lots of rattle on the rocks, not to mention talking high, wide an' truthfully to entire strangers by the wayside. You don't notice the I. B. C. posses doin' so when they're out on their own, do you? Only when they're with us. Remember the time we saw the camp-fire a mile away, an' that Lazy F puncher accidentally fired three shots?"

Mr. Henson digested this slowly.

"Seems to me this guy Arnold would be better dead, anyway," he observed.

"But I," returned Mr. Garfield, "should like to question him a little—if you don't mind. I'd like to hear any information he may wish to give against this International Beef Concern bunch that he was employed by when I first met him—and I'd like to know why he suddenly left 'em and switched over to the girl, and then why, havin' gone over to her side, he goes an'—does this kind of thing."

"Love with her," mumbled Mr. Henson, blushing.

"Oh, is that the explanation?" asked his chief with exaggerated relief. "Thank you so much! Thank you! Thank you! I should never have thought of that myself!"

Glancing at his deputy sidewise, and fearing lest

THE SAGE HEN

he take this sarcasm in good faith, Mr. Garfield became more explicit before relapsing into silence:

"It's altogether too damn foolish an explanation," he barked, "for me to think of when sober."

"Then again," said Mr. Henson, "where's this boy Grant?"

There was no answer. Mr. Garfield was indulging his age and annoyance in a sulk.

On the evening of the seventh day, as has been told, the Circle R ranch buildings burned—almost as completely and rapidly as though somebody had drenched them with gasoline and applied matches at a dozen points. As has further been said, Joan Bruce, from her sentry-guarded eyrie, saw it burn and became a little paler and more furious as she watched the last differentiation between her property and the surrounding prairie disappear in flame and smoke.

What has not been said is that John Arnold, on his sick-bed, heard of the bonfire; and through the rest of that night lay wide awake, his arms under his aching head, and—thought.

Sloan's bullet had not touched him; what ailed the big man with the clear gray eyes was something far more serious than the wound of any bullet ever made—assuming the bullet to have failed to inflict instantaneous death. He was suffering from the cumulative effect of long-continued strain, mostly under the shadow of death, and culminating in the superhuman exertions of the three days following his arrival in Texas from south of the Rio Grande. There exists a fiction to the effect that only white-collar men, sissies, office workers, can suffer from the complaint which was parching Arnold's throat and brain, making his heart race and his fingers twitch at the slightest sudden noise; but as a matter of fact, the class most subject to it is that comprising the he-men who live with a gun in the front of their pants, the law behind them and in front of them—nothing but a hole in the ground. As was proved in the war; for it was the snapping of the nerves under excessive strain; nervous breakdown; shell-shock—which had dropped Arnold from his saddle into the abyss of hot wretched unconsciousness in which he had remained, babbling and tossing, for two days and nights.

Now, all he wanted to do was to lie on his back, for ever more; never do anything; never say anything; never hear anything, never see anything except the sky through the branches above him; just to be let alone for the rest of eternity. He was tired—so tired that it seemed as though any exertion must kill him; yet, thinking over this news of the burning of the ranch house, he perceived that some kind of action was up to him. The I. B. C. had attacked the Sage Hen when she was under his protection, and sick or well, he was bound to counter-attack. The fighting instinct is the last of man's numerous funny little characteristics to leave him. When a dying man stops fighting death, he is dead.

But what was to be done?

It was with this problem, which eluded him, almost solved itself, escaped again, and dissolved itself into a million elements which his weary mind had to bring together again, that the sick leader wrestled during the long night hours; while the gang that awaited his orders slept loudly around the ashes of the fire which, in these perilous days, they had learned to put out before the sky was dark enough to reflect its glow.

Once, just as he seemed to be on the verge of capturing an idea, he heard the man with the B. S. A.

THE SAGE HEN

rifle, whose beat included supervision of Joan Bruce's leaf hut, say gently, "Mustn't go down there, miss"—and the idea took wings and fled. In its place, there crowded in upon him a wonder as to why the Sage Hen made no answer; where she had been going; what she thought of him; and then—a maddening puzzle which persisted for centuries, it seemed. He wondered what B. S. A. stood for. English rifle, judging by the caliber. Then the B would probably be for British—

The mysterious letters danced before his eyes in letters of fire, until only the fear of loss of the dignity which enabled him to command his gang of roughs prevented him from calling the sentry in and demanding the solution. Suddenly—for no reason—the imaginary letters disappeared.

Equally suddenly—for no reason—John Arnold knew, not only what he was going to do to the International Beef Concern, but exactly how he was going to do it. He was not excited by this sudden inspiration; the idea seemed so obvious—so simple—so perfectly natural that he had an odd feeling he had thought of it long ago, and just remembered it again.

THE SAGE HEN

There were no details to be thought out—the scheme was complete down to the last letter. Without changing his position or consciously removing his gaze from the Southern Cross which gleamed into his eyes through the screen of leaves that formed the roof, Arnold stopped thinking and slid into fifteen hours of sleep.

When he woke, it was dusk—six o'clock in the evening. He saw this with satisfaction as he got into his now strangely unfamiliar clothes, and donned hat and gun belt.

The elderly man, bearing a steaming pannikin of squirrel meat, met him as he emerged from the low entrance of the hut, and was amazed, almost to the point of dropping the dish.

"All ready?" asked Arnold.

The elderly man stared from the resurrected leader to the gaping rank and file about the fire.

"Why, y-yes, boss. Wh-what for?" he asked.

"In an hour's time," said Arnold, taking the pannikin, "we're going down to Hurst Seat, to—"

Then he stopped; for his gaze had just met that of Joan Bruce.

She had left her hut, crossed the intervening

space, and was now standing behind the elderly man; who, after a glance over his shoulder into those blazing eyes, stepped politely aside.

"Well?" said the Sage Hen.

Arnold fumbled with the brim of his hat, and removed it.

"Well, Miss Joan?" he asked.

Under the gaze of the girl, and that of his men, clustered immobile and staring around the fire, the newly pallid face of the big man began to flush—slowly, painfully.

"Are you satisfied now," the girl demanded, through clenched teeth, "you common traitor?"

The elderly bandit, with no very clear idea in his mind except that this was no way to address a sick man, took a step forward; then stopped. There was something rather attention-gripping in this bearding of a man whom all these ruffians feared, by a mere girl; but what stopped the elderly man in his tracks was the sight of John Arnold's face.

"I'm no traitor, Miss Joan," came the steady answer.

The girl laughed.

"No? Why not? What more is there for you to

do? You killed my brother; you lost our stock for us—all that was left of it; you captured the Circle R so that your—employers—could burn it; now you've got me for your prisoner. Why don't you make me sign the deed of sale—if you can?"

Arnold raised a shaking hand to his brow. The elderly man, still staring, swore internally—a startled, incredulous oath. The steely eyes of the boss had become more like those of an appealing dog than anything else in the elderly man's experience— which had been extensive. And—

"If that'd been what I'd—brought you away for," Arnold was saying, "we'd scarcely have been running around these hills for the last week, keeping you away from the beef company's men, would we?"

"From posses—after you—for murder!" cried the girl.

Nothing that could have been said would have convinced her of her error; but from around the fire there came a chorus of bitter chuckles that conveyed unmistakable truth.

Suddenly, the girl took a step backward.

"Then," she cried, with a new terror in her tone, "then why—did you bring me here?"

"So's the I. B. C. *shouldn't* get you."

"But—"

There was really every excuse for the conclusion to which, in that instant, the Sage Hen's mind leaped; good excuse aside, entirely, from the license for wild imaginings which was granted by the dusk, the loneliness and the peril of that rocky valley. This man before Joan Bruce, looming exaggeratedly large and terrible in the dim light, had fought the International Beef Concern, and made it miss its objective; contradictorily, he had fought and captured her. Obviously, then, he was neither on her side, nor in the employ of the I. B. C. He must be fighting for his own hand. And the only prize he could win in such a fight, the prize he had won—was Joan Bruce!

"Oh!" whispered the girl. "Oh, my God!"

She could just make out, in the gray eyes turned upon her, the expression which had paralyzed the elderly man.

"I—I can't do much explaining just now, Miss Joan," said Arnold slowly and uncertainly; "but—I aim to be your friend."

"My friend!"

She stepped up to him in the dusk.

THE SAGE HEN

"You cowardly dog!" she cried. "You wretched, treacherous dog! You, my friend! Listen. I fought off those thugs in the valley—until—you sold me out; there were hundreds of them. Do you think—"

She swung around on the men by the camp-fire.

"And you—you men!" she said scornfully. "You help him in this business—woman-stealing! A score of you—men!"

They flinched.

"I didn't sign on for that," said the man with the B. S. A. rifle slowly.

"And you've done none of it!" rang out Arnold's voice, suddenly changing its tone. "Who says you have? Come on. Let any one stand up and say I've double-crossed this gang, and led you into danger for my own purposes. By God, the man that says it, I'll kill!"

"I say it!" cried the girl. "Now kill me!"

Arnold turned toward her wearily, the revolver he had drawn hanging loosely in his hand.

"I was talking to—my men," he said gently.

"You'd better make good your threat to me," said Joan Bruce. "For if you don't—"

Her speech, high and hysterical, was interrupted.

In a voice almost as unsteady as her own, John Arnold broke in.

"You'll kill me when you get the chance?" he cried. "Then here—take this gun! Now, if you feel that way, for God's sake shoot me! Go ahead! I'm tired; I'm tired. You and your beastly suspicions! Go ahead! Fire!"

The man who had the foreign rifle and the wrist-watch and who now, as previously stated, keeps a cigar store in Chicago—is rather hazy about the exact termination of this rather interesting scene; he says he was too excited or something, to notice anything very minutely; and besides, the light was bad. He thinks, however, that Joan Bruce did raise the muzzle of the revolver which Arnold thrust into her hand; put her finger around the trigger, and pulled until the hammer of the double-action was almost at the falling point. In fact, on second thoughts, he is sure she did; because he remembers watching it rise, and wondering what prevented him from leaping to grab the girl's arm.

But no shot was fired.

Instead, the Sage Hen dropped the gun, and bursting into tears, stumbled, running over the

THE SAGE HEN

rocks to her hut. Arnold picked up the fallen weapon and replaced it in his holster. Then he stood there, silent and motionless, until the elderly man, clearing his throat, asked him if he was ready.

"Ready for what?" asked the leader, in a peculiar hoarse voice.

"Ready for this ride you said we was goin' on. Say, you feelin' sick again, boss? You don't seem right to me."

"Ride?" said John Aronld mistily. "Ride we were going on? Oh . . . yes. To Hurst Seat. Yes."

"Hurst Seat?" whispered one of the men about the fire. "Hurst Seat? Us? Now? He's crazy!"

The elderly man spoke gently.

"Would it help any to let us know what we're goin' for, boss?" he asked. "Sounds kind of a dangerous proposition, you see, an'—an' you haven't been—just yourself."

Arnold laughed.

"I'm not crazy," he said. "We're going down to Hurst Seat to play our trump card in the game."

"Well, what's the game?" asked a voice from the other side of the fire. "I've lost track of it."

THE SAGE HEN

"The game," said John Arnold clearly, "is to make the International Beef Concern, which wants the Circle R ranch, pay Miss Joan Bruce a proper price for it; so that she can get out of this mess without being killed or—worse. I thought we could fight 'em off. Well, we can't. This is the only way out."

There was an amazed and reflective pause.

"An' you think," said the man with the wrist-watch, "that we can do that—to-night?"

His tone was pitying.

"I know I can try it," snapped John Arnold. "You can come or not—as you like."

They went with him, slowly, hopelessly, reluctantly, like men riding to their deaths, and rather puzzled as to why they were doing it.

They returned in the gray of the next dawn, slowly, wearily, but in triumph.

For, hanging across the crupper of John Arnold's horse; conscious; unhurt; still clad in the suit of mauve silk pajamas he had been wearing when rough hands had snatched him from his bed in the Hurst Seat Hotel—they brought with them the person of Mr. William Rigby.

THE SAGE HEN

In the town itself, half-dressed men with sleep-bleared eyes and rifles in their hands, were wondering what to do in view of a notice they had found when they roused at the alarm.

It was a crude piece of sign painting—done with a charred stick on the back of an old circus poster; and it had been nailed to a telegraph pole where the light from a street lamp would make it most visible.

It read:

I. B. C. MEN!
We've got your boss
DON'T FOLLOW!

CHAPTER XVI

IT WAS—as Mr. William Garfield did not fail to point out when his opinion and aid were invoked —a slightly amusing situation; at which, nevertheless, he himself failed to laugh or even smile. He did the next best thing, however, by sitting in the foyer of the Hurst Seat Hotel, beneath the shade of a moth-eaten artificial palm, and explaining the joke painstakingly to each successive delegate imploring his assistance.

"You want me to do something?" Mr. Garfield asked, at least six separate times in the course of that confusing, hurrying, scurrying, terrified day, as he sat, hands on gun butts, his peg-leg crossed perkily over his good knee. "Well, what? Gimme a little suggestion. Let's hear from you. Just what is it you'd like me to do? Take action, you say. All right, what action?"

Receiving, in each case, no coherent answer to this question, the old gentleman launched every time upon a brief and mocking lecture.

THE SAGE HEN

"See?" he inquired. "See? You were all-fired smart, weren't you? You didn't need my help—not you. You could run your own illegal business your own illegal way. You wouldn't let me organize a proper hunt, would you? You wasted my time, an' flushed my game for me, didn't you? And now you want me to get your boss back for you, don't you? Well, I can't. If you'd let me alone, I'd have had that bunch surrounded and ready for capture— captured—three days ago. Now, if we go blunderin' after them, we may catch 'em or we may not; but anyway, Rigby'll be dead."

"Well, what are we goin' to do?" asked the foreman of the Lazy F, who headed the delegation which sought audience at two in the afternoon.

Mr. Garfield had been joined at dinner by Jake Henson and was now enjoying a leisurely cigarette. He finished the last few puffs before replying.

"Why, I'd wait patiently until your boss gives you your orders," he then advised sweetly. "Arnold's probably tellin' him what orders to give you."

But he was wrong.

It was not until four o'clock—until just about the hour, in fact, at which Jake Henson, looking thoughtful, left the Hurst Seat Hotel and rode rapidly toward Three Pines—that Mr. Rigby received any serious attention from his captors. In the first place, a wandering International Beef posse, which had been out all night and was not aware of the notice on the telegraph pole, forced a sudden change of camp. This, with the finding of a new location, consumed the whole morning. In the second place, even the most determined of desperadoes must sleep, and from noon on, having lashed Mr. Rigby to a pinnacle-like rock, all the gang save three sentries —two squatting at the prisoner's bare feet, and one on an eminence whence he could survey all approaches to the new retreat—the gang slept.

Joan Bruce was awake, too. In fact, it was the sight of her, sitting under a hastily-thrown-up version of her former branch shelter, that roused Mr. Rigby from the trance of incredulous terror which had heretofore paralyzed his brain, and fixed his rat-like eyes in his head.

The girl's expression was not one of triumph; rather, she seemed puzzled—painfully puzzled. She did not look like one whose enemy has been delivered into her hands. One would have thought, in fact, that she was wondering whether or not she had made some terrible mistake, and she really was wondering just that; but not for the reason Mr. Rigby assigned as he watched her. The subject of her thoughts was John Arnold, but it was the prisoner's opinion, based on a considerable experience of bullying women, that, having struck a return blow at her tormentors, this poor soft thing was feeling remorse and terror. Mr. Rigby's heart rose perceptibly.

There'd be no tortures or killing, after all, and with a few easily-broken promises, he could regain his freedom. And then—

The two sentries near him were talking in low tones, and overhearing their words, the breast under the mauve silk pajamas expanded still more.

"If she sells this here ranch," one man was asking the other, "what about those jobs he promised us?"

There was a pause before the other man replied.

"Well, I guess we'll see," he said uncertainly.

"Yeah—after we've done our stunt. Say, I dunno why I fell for this respectability stuff anyhow; an' if this guy leaves us holdin' the bag—"

"He won't!"

THE SAGE HEN

"Dunno about that!"

Mr. Rigby drew a deep breath.

"Boys!" he said in a whisper.

The men did not hear him; which was annoying, because Joan Bruce, who had moved away from her wikiup, and was staring into the reddening west, might turn around at any moment, and Mr. Rigby wished to speak to his guards quite privately.

"Well, anyhow," said one of the sentries, "this is the last shot in the locker. He holds four aces now, an' if he don't cop the pot—well, I ain't sittin' in on the next hand. Don't see anythin' in the business anyhow, win or lose—for us. To hell with this chivalry business, I say."

"Me, too," said the other man gruffly.

It was really unfortunate that Rigby had so low an opinion of the people with whom he dealt so largely; because if he had studied cowboys as human beings, instead of considering them merely to be pawns in his games, he would have recognized that gruffness for what it was—the quite false attempt of very sentimental men to prove themselves tough unfeeling nuts; and he would have saved himself a headache.

THE SAGE HEN

"Boys!" he whispered again; and when his guards turned to look at him, added hastily. "Ten thousand each if you'll cut me loose and give me ten minutes' start!"

He saw one sentry look at the other, as if in mute question; he thought his offer was being considered; and then, suddenly, one of the men stepped up and dealt him a most appalling smack in the face.

"Try to bribe me, you swine?" he heard a voice say, apparently from behind a sky full of shooting stars.

"An' me?" growled the other man.

Into Rigby's ears, past the sound of the bells which had been set ringing by the bang of his head against the rock, there came the voice of Joan Bruce, crying, "Stop, you cowards!" And what was more important, there came into his field of vision, flashing out of the fog as it cleared from his eyes, a long khaki-clad arm, which stopped a second stunning slap in mid-career.

Sick and dazed, the man in the mauve silk pajamas perceived himself to be surrounded by the whole population of the camp. To his left, flushed and furious, stood the Sage Hen, hands clenched, eyes blazing; in front of him, shrinking from the blast of the girl's rage, stood the two sentries; to his right, John Arnold was lowering the arm which had guarded Rigby's face. All around, the just awakened bandits looked on—a most unpleasant crowd.

"You—cut this man—loose and—let him go!" said Joan Bruce breathlessly. "You—miserable—bullying coward, you! Let him go at once!"

There was a considerable pause; and then John Arnold spoke in a most surprising way.

"Miss Bruce," he said coldly, but with a tremor in his voice which caused Rigby—and others too—to shiver suddenly. "I must tell you that my risking my life in your service does not give you the right to treat me as a servant."

The girl, her lips parted for another denunciation, gasped and became silent as she met those gray eyes.

"Do you understand that?" asked John Arnold.

"I can't understand any—brutality—or cowardice," the girl broke out defiantly. "You claim to be doing this for me—at least, I suppose you do. Then I have a right to say what shall be done in my name,

THE SAGE HEN

and I won't have a bound man beaten, or a helpless man bullied into—"

"Into what? Making amends for the damage he's done you?"

"That or anything else!"

Arnold beckoned two men.

"Take her away!" he said.

"How dare you!"

"Miss Bruce," said the big man slowly. "I've something to say to you; and since you force me, I'll say it now. You think this fighting business is fun. Yes, you do—in the bottom of your heart. Well, it ain't; at least, not to me; nor to any of these men. This isn't sport. This is life or death. You've been brought up soft, but you think you know it all. Lots of women do—an' it gets men killed. Down on the ranch, there, you were leadin' those punchers—an' that boy Grant—to certain death, because you were too proud to knuckle under. Now, after we've risked our lives helping you win this scrap, you want us to throw everything away and put our necks in nooses, because we're not acting lady-like. We're not ladies, Miss Bruce. We're men. Fighting's men's business; you've interfered in it enough. Take her away."

THE SAGE HEN

"My punchers and—Grant—were my business," cried the Sage Hen. "It was you who interfered. If you didn't like the business, why didn't you stay out?"

Very slowly, the well-remembered flush crawled up Arnold's cheeks.

"Take her away," he repeated in a low voice.

"I won't go!" cried the Sage Hen. "Now—tell your men to drag me. You murderer!"

"Don't blame—me—if you don't like—what you see—staying here," said the big man slowly.

Then, sharply, to his men:

"Cut Rigby loose."

With quick slashes of knives, they released the Viceroy of Hurst County from his bonds and led him, staggering, over to where Arnold sat upon a flat rock, the sunset behind him.

"On his knees!" said the big man quietly.

For some reason, however, all the stiffening seemed to have departed from Mr. Rigby. Left to kneel by himself, he fell forward on his face; and, in this position, began to weep bitterly. Joan Bruce, heartsick with distaste and anger, turned away.

THE SAGE HEN

"I said 'On his knees'!" came the quiet voice. "Get up, Rigby!"

There was a dead silence.

"Get up!" cracked the voice, and immediately, little stones rattled under apologetically scuffling hands.

"My God!" blubbered Rigby. "Don't kill me!"

Joan Bruce wondered how the semicircle of men could laugh; but then, of course, she had not seen the youngest member of this ragged army of hers shot dead by one of Rigby's bodyguard.

"We won't kill you," said Arnold slowly. "You know what you're here for?"

"Y-yes—I—c-can guess."

"What is it?"

Silence.

"Answer me, you dog!"

"I'm a h-hostage."

"I'm glad you realize it," said Arnold silkily. "I was afraid you might still think you were somebody with gunmen behind you, and money, and judges and such things. Yes, you're a hostage. You're all alone in the mountains, Mr. Rigby. Are you afraid?"

"N-no!"

Arnold looked at the cringing figure and laughed; on the other three sides of the wretched captive, the rest of the gang chuckled like wolves with an amusing bone.

"Then I guess it's no use asking you to write the letter I was thinking of asking you to write. Jack—"

The figure of the man with the B. S. A. rifle loomed up from among the sitting men.

"Yes, boss?" And, on the heels of the last word, came the slithering click of the bolt action.

"Oh, God!" shrieked Rigby.

"Are you afraid?"

"Yes! Yes!"

A pencil and a pad of the Hurst Seat Hotel's stationery clittered and flapped on the flat rock before him.

"Then write," said John Arnold.

Rigby dabbed for the pencil with fingers that refused to clutch, got it at last, and sat in a ghastly travesty of one taking dictation. Behind the figure of Arnold, as he squatted Buddha-wise on the rock, the sky had become a brilliant crimson, streaked

THE SAGE HEN

with long bars of bright gold. The grandeur of the heavens, plus the terror of this dark scene whose principal actor was silhouetted against the blaze, seemed to have had a hypnotic effect on Joan Bruce; for when Arnold addressed her, she answered without bitterness.

"How much was your ranch worth, before the I. B. C. wanted it?"

"One hundred thousand dollars."

Arnold considered.

"Since you're selling," he remarked, "you can't give these men the jobs I promised them. They'll need money instead."

Slowly recovering her senses, Joan Bruce laughed.

"I don't want money," said one of the men, shamed by her mockery.

"You do," said John Arnold. "You want to go straight, don't you? You can't, without money."

"Then I'll go crooked."

"You joined me to get a chance to come back," said John Arnold. "I promised it to you, and you'll have it, all of you—one thousand each. Jack, count heads. How many are there?"

THE SAGE HEN

"Nineteen—*now*," said the bandit who had sidekicked with the boy who lay dead in Hurst Seat.

"That's counting me," said Arnold. "I'm not in on this. Eighteen thousand dollars, then. That's a hundred and eighteen thousand."

"Why leave yourself out?" sneered Joan Bruce.

Arnold looked at her.

"Because I'm not doing this for money," he said.

"For—fun, then?"

"No. I don't fight—for fun."

"Then what are you doing it for?"

The man on the rock drew a hissing breath.

"Isn't that—my business?" he inquired softly.

Joan Bruce's heart stood still. Her fears were confirmed, then. She was his share of the plunder! She stood frozen, incapable of the speech which boiled within her.

"One hundred and eighteen thousand dollars, Rigby," said the quiet voice, "delivered to William Garfield, sheriff of Three Pines County,—in cash; to be deposited by him in the name of Miss Bruce, in the Acacia National Bank. When he has made this deposit, he will go to Five Mile and raise his arms above his head twice; we shall see him; and you'll be released."

THE SAGE HEN

"They won't pay it!" screamed Rigby.

"Won't they? Take the pencil."

"They'll let you kill me! What do they care?"

"Write what I tell you."

"I can't see. Oh, they'll laugh at it. They'll say, 'Go ahead—kill him.' What do they—"

Arnold struck a match.

"I don't know how you address them," he said, getting a long chain of matches ready for successive lighting, "but start the usual way. 'Dear Sirs,' for instance. Got that down?"

The pencil scratched clumsily.

"They know we've got you. Needn't write that. Now say, 'You must deposit one hundred and eighteen thousand dollars in cash'—have you got that?"

"They won't do it," blubbered Rigby, writing. "They'll tell you to kill me. I've seen them do it before. I—"

"Write! Have you got that?

"'—with William Garfield, sheriff of Three Pines within—' Where's the nearest headquarters?"

"Longhorn City. But—"

"Two days, then. 'Within two days.' Got that?

217

THE SAGE HEN

'This is the purchase price of the Circle R ranch'—got that? Now what's the legal phrase 'including all standing buildings and stock on the hoof?' Yes, put that in. That'll make 'em laugh."

Rigby himself essayed a feeble titter; but it eventuated as sobs.

" 'To be deposited in the name of Joan Bruce'—write where."

The third match flared.

" 'After which deposit, Garfield will ride to Five Mile and raise his arms twice as a signal. I shall then be released.' "

"B—but if they refuse?"

"They—won't refuse."

"They will! There was Mr. Edwards, over near Corpus Christi—they let him be killed!"

Sobs choked Rigby's utterance again.

"But I'm cleverer," said Arnold very gently, "than the men who killed Mr. Edwards. . . . You've served the I. B. C. a long and dirty time, haven't you?"

"Yes, but—"

"You've been on the inside of a lot of little steals like this—bossed a lot of gunmen and so on, haven't you? You know the I. B. C. pretty well, don't you?"

The unfortunate victim's voice was a whisper.

"I know—well enough—know they'll let you—"

"Never mind about that. You know a lot of things that they wouldn't—want known, don't you?"

"Yes!" moaned Rigby. "They'd be glad to have me—"

Arnold leaned forward across the flat rock and gripped the prisoner's wrist.

"Look at me!" he said between his teeth.

Rigby raised his swollen rat's eyes to the grim, shadow-darkened face above him. Its expression, intensified by the gleam, in the darkness, of the white of the eyeballs and of the teeth, threw him into a violent shuddering fit.

"Are you—afraid?" hissed the quiet voice.

"Yes! Y-yes!"

"Are you very afraid, Rigby?"

A choking sob.

"Are you afraid—for your life?"

"Aaaah!" screamed the Viceroy of Hurst County. "Ah, don't kill me! O God, have mercy on me. Don't!"

THE SAGE HEN

In a frenzy of horror, he dashed the hand which Arnold was not holding across his eyes, and stumbled to his feet. And, standing, he babbled in idiotic shrieks until Joan Bruce, paper-white, staggered for support against a rock; and even the tough men of the gang licked their dry lips and turned their eyes away.

In the middle of which scene Arnold, grim and self-contained, struck another match and flung Rigby down again at his stone desk.

"Then you'll write these two words just as I want 'em written," he added, through his teeth. "Are you ready?"

Mechanically, Rigby clutched the pencil.

"Write," said Arnold, "under your signature, just these two words—"

He paused and glanced around as though inviting his men to puzzle over the two words that could be expected to bring the International Beef Concern to its knees, when cold steel, hot lead and warm blood, had failed. In the orange-red flare of the match, his smiling face seemed positively diabolical.

"What—are the words?" gasped Rigby.

"Write—*'I'll tell.'* "

CHAPTER XVII

IN VIEW of what was publicly alluded to as "Mr. William Rigby's long record of faithful service," or, in the privacy of the International's board room as "the swine's inside dope"; also in view of the eagerness of a certain congressional committee, then sitting, for any scandalous news about the Beef Concern—it was decided to swallow the bitter pill and fulfill the conditions of the letter which had been found nailed to the Longhorn City office door.

A last attempt was made to bribe Mr. William Garfield to appear at Five Mile and give the prearranged signal, in consideration of one thousand dollars to himself, instead of one hundred and eighteen thousand deposited to the credit of Joan Bruce. This attempt failed; Mr. Garfield making a quiet polite refusal which was much more galling than the rage which might have been expected.

"It must seem funny to you," snarled the I. B. C. official who had made this proposal, "an elected

THE SAGE HEN

peace officer—to be acting as a murderer's collection agent."

"Joan Bruce is no murderer," replied the aged sheriff peaceably. "I'm collectin' for her. Anyhow, the funniest thing is me actin' as a hired thug's ransom-bearer—if you are lookin' for humor. An' anyway, I won't ride to Five Mile an' be a traitor."

"One hundred thousand dollars," muttered the official, motioning to an armed man, guarded by two others, who carried a steel-lined bag.

"Somebody phoned me night before last, and said one hundred and eighteen thousand," Mr. Garfield remarked gently. "Try any more monkey business, an' I won't go to Five Mile at all."

And in point of fact, though the hundred and eighteen thousand was duly deposited in the Acacia National Bank, he never did go to Five Mile.

Instead, at three o'clock that afternoon, he arose from behind a rock, peg-legged his way carefully down a slope of shifting stones and, faced by a dozen open mouths of rifles and men, brought the news to John Arnold in person.

"Bill Garfield!" screamed the Sage Hen.

"Don't fire!" boomed John Arnold's voice at the same instant.

222

THE SAGE HEN

There was a silence of paralytic surprise; in which the little, frail old man, standing there scratching his alkali-dusted gray whiskers, with no hand near his guns, spoke diffidently.

"I just thought," he remarked, "that, having my duty to attend to, and my oath of office, an' all that, p'raps I'd better come myself. There's so many things can't be done by wigwag."

The man with the B. S. A. rifle clucked convulsively in his throat. Mr. Garfield's eyes swung to him unerringly; it almost seemed as though he was watching the little lift of the cocking-piece as the half-bent began to press against the scear.

"Now, now," he said mildly.

It seemed perfectly unreal—like some kind of fantastic dream. Around, for miles, stretched and climbed the rugged hills, with their millions of wild volcanic seams; in the midst of this desolation, under the free blue sky, were gathered nearly a score of desperate men, all armed, all perfectly willing to kill at the bat of an eyelash. By the simple process of moving camp, and keeping quiet, they had for many days eluded capture with the greatest ease; from their position of invisibility among the crags, they, a handful, had struck a world-wide organization a vital blow. That one aged man should dare to come among them—alone, and with no apparent disposition to use force—and that, being there, he should have the power to make every man present feel that the game was up, was, by all theory, absurd.

Yet so it was.

"The—money's—been paid?" asked a hoarse whisper.

The eyes of the gang, detaching themselves from the face of old Bill Garfield with a difficulty suggestive of hypnotism, turned on John Arnold. He was standing near Mr. Garfield, and it was to be noticed that while every muscle of every other man present was contracted to the limit of tautness, the shoulders of the leader had a little droop that was new; moreover, his long powerful arms hung with a peculiar limpness. His whole body seemed relaxed.

"Yes," said Mr. Garfield. "The money's paid. It's in the bank to Miss Bruce's credit. I was thinkin' of taking her down to sign the deeds and what's-his-names. Might as well take Rigby down, too. I don't suppose you boys'll mind bein' relieved of that trouble."

THE SAGE HEN

What was there about that speech to make a cold shiver visit the spine of the elderly man? Soon, he identified the ingredient. Old Bill Garfield had not spoken to John Arnold; more than that, he had pointedly looked away from him, and at the rest of the bunch, when he uttered the words "You boys." Like a chill wind, there swept into the elderly man's consciousness a clear idea that Arnold was being separated, in point of treatment, from the rest of them, being cut out of the herd, as a mad bull is separated from his companions.

The elderly man got to his feet. His eyes and the eyes of Mr. Garfield met in perfect understanding. Then Mr. Garfield coughed, and a rifle-barrel slid quietly over the top of a flat rock behind him. Nobody saw it but the elderly man; and, a moment later, John Arnold.

"Ah—h'mmm!" repeated Mr. Garfield, covering up his signal-cough. "H'mmm. The afternoon air. At this elevation. Well, if you're ready—"

"You ain't—come here—for all of us—alone?" said the man with the sporting rifle—in a powdery, whispering voice.

"Not alone," said Mr. Garfield. "No, not alone.

THE SAGE HEN

Dessay I got fifty—sixty men 'round the base of this hill. I just came up with Jake Henson so's not to alarm you-all. That's Jake behind the rifle-barrel. . . . You see, I don't want any of you boys, an'—I thought if I came alone, we might save —misunderstandings."

Now the exclusion of John Arnold from the remarks applying to the rest of the gang was unmistakable. Everybody got it. And everybody, with a sudden movement, got to his feet.

"Down!" shouted John Arnold. "Put those guns down!"

"Jake," said Mr. Garfield, slowly and clearly, "put the whistle in your mouth, but don't blow it."

He turned, now, for the first time, and faced Arnold. He said no word; he knew too well how much more certainly the names of things control human reactions, than do the things themselves. Had he uttered the word "murder," or gone through the formal motion of arrest, he would have been a dead man that instant. So he raised his bushy old eyebrows at John Arnold just the fraction of an inch; and saw the big loose-jointed man before him nod very slightly; while the gang, poised on the

THE SAGE HEN

point of killing, watched with doubt-dulled comprehension.

Then, suddenly, something went wrong. By some inspiration, some trick of the brain, one man received a flashing revelation of what was going on, and what it meant. It meant that one of themselves, and he no less than the chief, was being taken away to certain death at the hands of the law, while they stood by and made no protest.

The man uttered a low growl of fury; and instantly, like electric machines whose switch has been touched, the whole score of men swept forward toward Bill Garfield.

Jake Henson's breath, indrawn, hissed through the passages of his whistle; his finger tightened on the trigger; but before the breath could be expelled in a shrill blast that should bring fifty Three Pines men up, before the finger could send the first of six bullets thudding into the mass—John Arnold had leaped forward and stopped the rush with uplifted hand.

"Get back!" he roared; and his hand flashed to his belt. "Get back, till I've done talking with you. You fools! Get back! . . . Now, listen. We've been together in this business. It wasn't any business of yours. It was of mine. You joined me because—you were sick of being on the outside edge. You wanted to come back. Well, you're back now. We've won this fight, and it's something to be proud of; there's a thousand for each of you in the Acacia National Bank. With pride and a thousand dollars, any man can—start a decent life."

Mr. Garfield, standing behind his prisoner, nodded to himself.

"This—business—now," said Arnold slowly, "has nothing to do with you. This is an old story. I—"

"We knew about it when we joined you," growled one of the men. "We knew it while we stuck to you. Are we goin' to quit you for it now?"

"Not quit me for that!" cried Arnold. "That's not what you're quitting me for—and you're not quitting me. I'm firing you—I'm—I'm dismissing you with—thanks and—best wishes. You're quitting me because, if you don't, if you fight now and get killed, most of you, an' the rest jailed, you'll spoil—something I'm kind of proud about. See?"

The men stood, checked. Mr. Garfield, seem-

THE SAGE HEN

ingly puzzled, was combing his whiskers with gnarled old hands. It might have been noticed, had any one been in condition to notice, that the old gentleman's eyes were fixed on Joan Bruce; who, in turn, was staring at John Arnold with a most strange expression. It was her gaze, in fact, that was puzzling Mr. Garfield.

"All right then," said Arnold, "cut Rigby loose."

No one moved. Arnold stepped over, and slipping the revolver he had drawn back into its holster, cut Rigby free with his own knife. The Viceroy of Hurst County said nothing, though his beady eyes moved continually, with an expression of terrible malevolence, like those of a snake with a broken back.

"What are you arresting him for?" asked Joan Bruce, dazed.

Arnold became, suddenly, deadly pale.

Mr. Garfield combed his whiskers.

"I—er—" he began, and stopped. "I'm—er—just taking him along, my dear. You're coming, too."

"You're—arresting him—for my brother's murder!" cried the girl.

THE SAGE HEN

Mr. Garfield stopped combing his whiskers, endeavored to force a smile, and broke into a profuse perspiration.

"Oh—" cried Joan Bruce.

John Arnold's eyes were upon her; and, suddenly, as if drawn by them, she stretched out her hands ever so little, and took half a step toward him. Then, stopping, she hesitated, one hand at her throat; and, after an instant, turned toward the hesitant gang. One arm she flung in the air, as if, in another second, she would urge them to the rescue; to the aid of this murderer with the gray eyes, to the annihilation of the law that was to work her revenge upon him.

But no words came.

Joan Bruce wavered, staggered, and then, before the widened eyes of the gang, dropped in a dead faint.

On the ride down to Hurst Seat, she rode, conscious but dazed, before Mr. William Garfield.

Occasionally, the aged sheriff would glance from the face against his shoulder to that of John Arnold, riding unmanacled and armed next to him, while Jake Henson and the posse jingled behind.

THE SAGE HEN

After each glance, Mr. Garfield scowled, drew a deep breath, and combed his whiskers as if in deep perplexity.

It was a perplexity so deep, and of such a peculiar kind, as to make him seem strangely unenthusiastic when, leaving Joan and Rigby at the hotel, he confined John Arnold in the Hurst Seat jail, on a charge of wilful murder.

Possibly it was this lack of enthusiasm, noticed by loungers, which resulted in the shocking attack by masked lynchers, upon the jail that night. Or possibly the I. B. C., burning for revenge, had issued secret instructions.

Mr. Garfield's own opinion of the cause of the attack—in which, by the way, the first man to fall was a gigantic negro—was that a rumor had suddenly begun to circulate; saying, with perfect truth, that since James Bruce's body had never been found, and since there was, accordingly, no *corpus delicti*—the law, so far from hanging John Arnold, would be compelled to dismiss him the moment he came to trial.

With the powder grime still black on his hands, Mr. Garfield tracked that rumor to its source.

THE SAGE HEN

It had originated, he found—and he combed his whiskers passionately at the discovery—with an attorney named Carstairs—who was Joan Bruce's lawyer!

CHAPTER XVIII

IT WAS a rather awe-inspiring sight to see the International Beef Concern reorganize and prepare to execute its revenge. Not a pleasant sight, any more than it would be pleasant to see a gigantic slimy snake, badly wounded by an exhausted hunter, turn and prepare to wrap its loathsome coils about its assailant, and crush him to death; but remarkable and fascinating in its way. Even Mr. William Garfield, who was opposed to such spectacles personally, as well as officially, found himself unable to do anything more than look on, with horrified interest, as Death closed in on John Arnold.

For more than a week, the I. B. C.'s loosely disciplined forces had been in utter confusion, culminating in a crushing, decisive and unexpected defeat; a defeat such as, in war, would have discouraged an army for months. Yet, within thirty-six hours, the counter-attack, designed—since it

THE SAGE HEN

could not recover the lost spoils of battle—to make a horrible example of the despoiler, was well under way, perfectly disciplined, perfectly organized and going fast.

In other words, the International Beef Concern was going to hang John Arnold by due process of law; nominally for the murder of one James Bruce; but actually, as everybody understood, for the more heinous crime of protecting one Joan Bruce against the concern's excellent and benevolent plans for its own benefit. Under such circumstances, legal quibbles about missing corpses and the lack of corroborative evidence were entirely beside the point; yet the I. B. C. honored them with its attention. Within four hours after giving his opinion on John Arnold's case, Mr. Attorney-at-Law Carstairs was persuaded to take an automobile ride with several perfect strangers who carried him off to Longhorn City and locked him in a room. Simultaneously, the two other lawyers in town, who would not have touched the defense end of the case with a long pole anyhow, were informed that since Arnold confessed the crime, and the district attorney, despite rumors to the contrary, had abundant corroborative evidence, any one attempting rebuttal would be injuring his professional career beyond repair.

Nor was this all.

The law, even when administered by a controlled district attorney, a privately-owned grand jury, a bought judge and a petty jury with no ideas of its own, is regrettably uncertain; a busy Trust is always faced with the possibility of having to correct the law's mistakes by violence. So that all the I. B. C. men from the outlying ranches were invited to spend a week or two in Hurst Seat, lounging around with their guns on, while the posse of Three Pines men which surrounded old Bill Garfield was gently and continually reminded of work at home, which was being neglected for the sake of this self-confessed double traitor who boasted of having murdered the man who had been his benefactor.

"I don't see," said Mr. Garfield, when the posse informed him that it was going home, "why you can't talk about the poor devil as the guy that saved Joan Bruce from—well, you know all about that. It's no use talking to you. Go on home if you want to."

"If there's another lynchin' bee, Bill," asked the

spokesman of the party, "who's goin' to protect you?"

Mr. Garfield stretched his peg-leg into the most brilliantly sunlit portion of the jail porch, and meticulously picked a splinter off it.

"There won't be another lynchin' bee," he remarked, chewing the splinter with his four remaining teeth. "That was just a burst of youthful spirits. He'll be hanged legally enough now. May say that I've never had a prisoner lynched on me yet, an' that if there was an attempt now, I dare say I could cope with it even without you-all; but there won't be one; so you can go mend your fences with cheerful minds."

"I don't know, Bill," said Two Toes Trotter. "Did you hear about this guy Grant comin' back to town? You know he was out all the time we were, lookin' for this Arnold to kill him with his bare hands. Last night, I seen him talkin' to those Circle R punchers—Sloan, and Corliss, an' the others. Looked bad to me."

Mr. Garfield rolled a cigarette.

"Well, stay if you feel so bad about it," he remarked casually.

THE SAGE HEN

"We don't feel bad about it on *his* account," snapped Two Toes. "It's on your score we feel bad, Bill; an' you ain't treatin' us right. We got work to do, an' you know it. You got no right to make us feel's though we ought to stay here with you, all on account of a dirty crawling thug that's so full of pep when he's winnin', an' now he's copped does nothing but sit in his cell with his head in his hands, an' say nothin'."

Suddenly, Mr. Garfield got to his feet. It was noticeable, furthermore, that as he did so, his antique ivory-colored cheeks flushed slightly, and that he permitted his cigarette to burn a crisp patch on the underside of his gray-white mustache.

"You just can that talk, Trotter," said the old man with unusual bruskness. "Now listen to me. I've been bitterer against James Bruce's killer than any of you-all; I am yet; an' when he's hanged, like he's goin' to be, I'll say he deserved it. A couple of weeks ago, I'd have said he deserved all these names you're pinnin' on him, an' all the maulin' an' burnin' them lynchers wanted to give him the other night; but now I don't say so, an' you shan't either. You're a bunch of young fellows yet, the whole of you, an' there's only one side to your ledger. Well, I'm old, an' there's two to mine—credit as well as debit. This jasper Arnold's got a whale of a debit, which he can't pay except by the rope; he's goin' to pay it. But he's got a whale of a credit, too—an' it ain't nice for you-all to forget it, either. Never mind about him getting into this mess defending Joan Bruce which you fellers talked about so much—an' never did. Just fix your minds on the fact that if he hadn't told that gang of his to lay back an' let him be arrested, there's a lot of you that wouldn't be here now."

"That's true," said a voice from the back of the posse.

Mr. Garfield sat down, stopped the gradual consumption of his whiskers by fire, and spoke more gently.

"Well, since you get that point of view, I don't mind takin' a load off your minds by sayin' that I've known you were goin' for longer than you have, an' that I've got a little posse to take your place."

"Who's in it?" demanded Two Toes Trotter jealously. "I. B. C. men, I'll bet, that'll shoot you in the back."

"Wrong," said Mr. Garfield. "I dunno all their names; but one's Sloan, another's Corliss, an' I think this guy Dave Grant's goin' to join us, too."

There was an incredulous silence.

"You—recruited—*them?*" asked Two Toes Trotter.

"No," said Mr. Garfield. "*She* did."

"The girl—he's in jail for killin'—her own brother?"

"No," said Mr. Garfield again, "the girl he got jailed rescuin' from the I. B. C."

"Oh," said Two Toes vaguely, and pawed the shifting dust before the prison steps with his toe.

"Yeah," said Mr. Garfield. "Still, kiddin' aside, you boys can drag your freight, now you ain't draggin' it under any misapprehension. It's all over, bar the hangin'. I don't count the trial; that'll be a farce. Ain't it funny, though, that when a guy says he killed a man, the law has to go to all the trouble of gettin' perjurers that wasn't even in the county at the time to swear they saw him do it, before he can be punished?"

"Have they done it?" asked Two Toes, feeling a little sick.

THE SAGE HEN

"You know the grand jury indicted Arnold this morning? Well, four I. B. C. men came an' swore they saw him kill James Bruce an' throw the body into Stony Springs Creek—all hacked." Mr. Garfield dropped his cigarette suddenly, reached for his jacket and rose again. "Say, you boys, hop it. If I need you, I'll send for you. Here's Miss Bruce coming, an' she don't want to walk through a crowd."

The Three Pines posse began to melt obediently. "When's the trial, Bill?" asked one of the men.

"To-morrow morning," said Mr. Garfield. "Now, on your way!"

CHAPTER XIX

IT HAS been said before that something in Joan Bruce's attitude toward the man who was at once her deadliest enemy and her best-proved friend, had puzzled Mr. Garfield; and he was still puzzled —very obviously so—as he stood on the prison porch, watching the backs of his Three Pines posse recede undecidedly, and the Sage Hen approach. His speech to the posse men on the subject of credit and debit balances had been taken from the body of his reflections concerning Joan Bruce; he had endeavored to convince himself, without any conspicuous success, that the girl's ledger consisted entirely of credit entries. Looking at her now, as she came up the steps to the porch, Mr. Garfield groaned internally and abandoned this idea for ever. This girl with the pale set face was not of the type to forget essential elements in a problem. Her speech, calm and collected, when she stood facing Mr. Garfield, supported this idea.

THE SAGE HEN

"The grand jury indicted him this morning?" she asked.

"For murder in the first degree," said the sheriff, bowing.

"Then," said Joan Bruce, a strange little tremble in her tones, "there must have been perjured evidence. The lawyer, Mr. Carstairs, told me that, without that, it would be impossible to convict him."

"There was perjury," said Mr. Garfield, nodding. "Lots of it."

"What did—Arnold—do?"

"Why, he laughed," said Mr. Garfield, looking at the girl, as if he expected sympathy. "Yes, miss, he sat back in his chair and he laughed."

The girl's small brown hands clenched.

"Does he want to be hanged?" she cried suddenly.

"Don't you—want him to be?" asked Mr. Garfield, a tinge of ice in his usually indulgent voice.

"No, I don't!"

"Your dead brother," said the old sheriff coldly, "might not be pleased to hear you say that, miss."

"My dead brother would understand what I mean," said Joan Bruce. "I mean that this John Arnold, whatever he's done, deserves a fair trial

THE SAGE HEN

and a fair chance for his life. He's earned it; and now it seems that earning it is just the reason why he's not going to get it. I want him dealt with according to law. I want him given justice. Now do you understand what I mean? If, in justice, he's to hang, let him hang. But—"

Mr. Garfield was nodding his comprehension—with reservations. The reservations were expressed, to one who knew how to read them, in the peculiar set of his wrinkled old lips under their growth of gray whiskers; and even more clearly in the penetrating, ice-blue stare of his crow's-footed, bright eyes.

"It's hard to see even—anybody—gettin' railroaded," he agreed softly. "But—what you goin' to do about it?"

The girl drew a sudden breath.

"I—" she began.

"The case," said Mr. Garfield, "ain't in your hands, you see. It's in the hands of the state, which is the same as to say, of the county, which is the same as to say, of the International Beef Concern. An' the International Beef Concern is goin' to hang this guy."

THE SAGE HEN

Yes, the girl winced at the word "hang." Mr. Garfield's watchful old eyes narrowed just a trifle more, and his upper lip seemed to lengthen just the tiniest trifle in the world.

"I—must see him," said Joan Bruce.

"Er—?"

"Alone!"

The sheriff stopped combing his whiskers, and actually rolled and lighted a cigarette without asking permission. In an ex-Texas Ranger captain of the old school, this was a sign of the last stage of mental agitation.

"You mean," he inquired, after a few agitated puffs, "that you want to see Arnold in his cell—alone?"

"I must see him," said the Sage Hen.

"It's imp—" began Mr. Garfield, and then stopped dead as the girl, her eyes suddenly filled with tears, clasped her hands before him. "Oh, lord! Now, now, missy. That'll be all right. It's against the rules, but—it's all right. I'll do it."

Turning hastily on the pivot of his peg-leg, he led the way into the jail; spun around again, three feet inside the door, stepped back into the sunlight,

THE SAGE HEN

and with agitated courtesy, let the girl enter first; then, stumping past her, regardless of all etiquette, he yelled stridently for the turnkey.

"Lady to the prisoner Arnold—an' then come here," he ordered, fixing this functionary with his eye.

"To the mur—"

"Where I said!" snapped Mr. Garfield.

A minute later, Arnold, sitting, staring wearily at the backs of his big brown hands, heard footsteps outside his cell door; raised his eyes to look listlessly at the indistinct figures showing through the bright steel bars of his cell; and then rose, suddenly tense, as the spring lock clicked, the door swung back, and Joan Bruce entered.

"Joan!" he cried.

The steel bars swung back into place, the heavy lock clicked again; the turnkey's footsteps died away; and he was alone with her. He saw that her cheeks, which had been pale, were now suddenly scarlet. He thought he knew why.

"I—mean—I was surprised to see you—Miss Bruce."

His eyes dropped before hers. He was really

awfully tired; not so much in body as—just tired. He hadn't had the energy—hadn't cared enough—to contradict the liars at the grand jury session that morning; now he hadn't the nerve, it seemed, to look this girl in the eyes.

Mr. Garfield was surprised at the silence which followed. It was intensely repugnant to his finer feelings, but a sheriff's office can not be run on sentiment; and, having a sworn duty, faithfully performed over fifty years, to the people of the state of Texas, Mr. Garfield was crushing down his personal likes and dislikes, and making as sure as he could that his prisoner was not being supplied with what are legally described as "the means to suicide, or implements calculated to assist in a delivery from jail." In other words, he was sitting at the other end of the corridor, eavesdropping.

"Mr. Arnold," said the voice of Joan Bruce.

The prisoner raised his head. "Yes, miss?"

"I've come to say that—I'm sorry."

"That's—all right, miss."

"Oh, don't speak like that!" cried the girl, half hysterically. "Why do you answer me like a—dead man?"

"Ow!" said Mr. Garfield to himself, wincing in the darkness of his end of the passage.

"Can't you see what I mean?" the girl stormed on. "I'm sorry for—what I thought of you—up there in the hills. I thought—I thought that——"

"You couldn't be blamed," said John Arnold slowly. "Though it wasn't so. I'd like you to— I'm glad you know that, Miss Joan. I was just figuring to see you didn't get robbed of your ranch, and so on; and I had to act kind of desperately."

"Why—did you do it?"

There was another of the silences Mr. Garfield disliked. He marked his disapproval by leaning forward, elbows on knees, and listening with peculiar intensity.

"Help you with your—ranch, you mean?"

"Yes, I've been thinking it over. If the Concern enlisted you in Mexico, you must have known— what it was for. You must have joined the I. B. C. in the first place—to help me."

There was no answer; but in the darkness, Mr. William Garfield nodded, his eyes narrowed to slits.

"Why did you do it?"

A short laugh.

THE SAGE HEN

"I'd something to make up to you, it seems to me," said John Arnold's voice huskily.

"Had you?"

"What—do you mean—Miss Joan?"

To his intense surprise, Mr. Garfield found his heart pounding in a very strange and unprecedented manner indeed. The blood, was, in fact, hammering in his head until his hearing was affected, and it was necessary for him muffling his peg-leg with his antique Stetson, to creep a considerable distance down the jail corridor before he could be sure that he could properly fulfil his duty. He crept so close, in his zeal, that he found himself within three feet of the cell door; actually able to hear Arnold's breathing, which seemed strangely loud.

"I mean this," said Joan Bruce, so close at hand that the listener shrank back a foot or so. "I hear that all the testimony against you is perjured. I—want to know the truth. Did you—kill my brother?"

The man's breath, thought Mr. Garfield, actually seemed to be rattling in his throat.

"I've told you—before," came the hoarse words.

"I don't believe it!"

"Why not?"

THE SAGE HEN

"I—don't believe—you could do it."

The accused man gave a bitter chuckle.

"I could bring a lot of competent witnesses," he said dully, "to assure you I'm the very man for the job."

"Then why did you do it?"

"That doesn't matter. I had reasons. Good reasons. And if it comes down to that, I—I did you a good turn—doing it. He was running away, like a cottontail rabbit, and leaving his men in the lurch, when I—"

"You lie!"

There was a terrible pause.

"Oh," said the man, in an odd breathless voice. "All right, then. I thought, maybe—"

"How dare you!" said Joan Bruce slowly. "How dare you say that! I—I've been wrong. I see that now. You cur! He helped you—put you on your feet—tried to make a man out of you. I thought—I thought—there might be some mistake, some noble reason for your saying that you'd—killed him. But if you can say that about him, you did kill him! Even his worst—open—enemies never said such a thing as that. He was a Bruce!"

THE SAGE HEN

Mr. Garfield, who for some reason was looking exceedingly excited, looked for one moment a little surprised at this. But then again, it was perfectly probable that the girl had never heard all the harrowing circumstances surrounding her brother's death. What she had to know, had been bad enough.

"Very well, then," said John Arnold.

"I'm going," said the girl. "I'm going. Let me go!"

The steel bars of the gate were new and would not rattle; but an instant later the electric bell boomed as the prisoner touched the call-button; and from the direction of the prison door, the turnkey's steps approached.

This worthy was looking forward, rather, to seeing tears and pale faces in the cell; but it was extremely shattering to his sense of the fitness of things to meet, at the end of the corridor, his aged superior, Mr. William Garfield, stumping along with exaggerated care to make no noise, exceedingly tattered-looking about the whiskers, apparently trembling all over, and clearly oblivious, for the moment, of the turnkey's existence.

Anybody might have thought the poor old duck

THE SAGE HEN

was crazy, in fact, the way he acted—rushing into the office of the lock-up, tearing open the records of prisoners received, and then rushing out of the jail for a destination unknown, leaving a great big unclean thumb-mark all over the line stating John Arnold's place of last abode.

It was Pueblo Indio, Chihuahua, Mexico, the turnkey noted, as, after showing Joan Bruce out of the prison, he returned the book indignantly to its rack.

By a strange coincidence, that was the identical place for which Mr. William Garfield's deputy, Jake Henson, was leaving Three Pines when, five hours later, in the darkness of the night, a voice under John Arnold's cell window called softly:

"Hey, Arnold! Are you awake?"

CHAPTER XX

HE WAS awake; both in the sense of not being physically asleep, and in the more unusual respect of having a clear, exact and unemotional idea of the circumstances surrounding him. The majority of men condemned to death—as John Arnold was, though his formal trial was still to come—have no difficulty whatever in keeping their eyes open during the long nights; but it is rare to find one who dares turn the eyes of his mind upon his situation and think and realize what it means. That way lies madness—for most of the men who find themselves condemned. The killer type is not designed to stand much agony of spirit. It was another puzzling trait in the character of John Arnold, however, that his reflections, since the visit of Joan Bruce, seemed to have calmed and strengthened him. When she had entered his cell, he had been a weary man, suddenly buoyed up by a new hope; when, furious, she had left him, he had sunk,

THE SAGE HEN

like a rock deprived of its buoy, to the very bottom of the sea of depression.

But during the dusky hours he had spent sitting upon his narrow cot under the high barred window, he had, instead of sinking into the primordial ooze of the sea aforesaid, seemed on the contrary to rise and swim upward by his own efforts. Certainly he had no help from without. Before his eyes, as he sat there, was nothing but heavy stone, mortised and mortared to keep him in; a chilled steel grille, gleaming uncompromisingly in the failing light; his ears brought him no sound more hopeful than the clang of the jail's main door as it was locked, bolted and barred for the night; and his mind can only have presented to him the knowledge that whereas his enemies, plotting in the gray of the evening, were as hot against him as ever, his only friend—for Joan Bruce had assumed this position for a little while—had turned against him.

Yet, by the time that voice called in through his cell window, John Arnold was himself again—himself as he had been before the desperate events of his invasion of Hurst County, had broken, as it were, his nerve; calm, grave, yet alert.

THE SAGE HEN

At the call, he rose suddenly from his seat.

"Yes?" he called softly. "Who's this?"

There was a pause, and then came the answer.

"David Grant. I've come to get you out of this."

With a smothered exclamation, Arnold sprang on his cot, and, with straining muscles, tried to look out through the little window. But the broad sill of stone prevented his seeing anything but the sky. There was no moon, but, straight before him, like Hope in the night of despair, there blazed the Southern Cross.

"You young fool," he began.

Below, sitting on his horse, Grant cut in on him.

"Listen, Arnold," he said. "There's no time for argument and fal-lals. I've got a hacksaw here, and a rope. That window's big enough to let you through. Your men are in town. They've promised us fifteen minutes free from interruption, and they'll ride with you when you're out. Can you hear me?"

"I hear you," said the low voice from the cell window.

"Well, then, don't fool away time arguing. I'm going to throw the saw up. Put your hand out."

THE SAGE HEN

Grant was already standing on his saddle, reaching upward, as he finished the sentence; but no hand appeared to take the saw whose point touched the coping of the window.

Instead:

"I'm staying here," said Arnold.

"Take the saw!" whispered the man on the horse vehemently. "You damned fool, do you think this is any fun for me? I've hunted you for a week, to kill you. Take the saw! Joan Bruce is in love with you, God help her."

"Have you seen her—to-day?"

"No—"

"Well, I have. Listen to me. You're wrong. She's—she was—kind of grateful for—my helping her. That's all. I thought for a minute, you might—"

"Love's not blinding me, Arnold. You killed her brother!"

"It's not blinding her, either. This—afternoon—she said she hoped I'd—hang. Can you hear me? Listen!"

"I——"

"Listen!"

There was a silence.

"Listen," said John Arnold slowly, his eyes on the distant star. "I'm going to tell you the truth, Grant. If one of my own men'd come for me, I'd have made a break. Since you came, I won't. And this is why. The girl loves you. Listen, you fool! She's hysterical, over this ranch business—figures she's a woman hero, an' all that; she thinks—thought a fighting man was the one for her. You fought—but you're not a fighting man. You're the kind of man she ought to marry, thank God—and now this is all over, she'll see it. Listen! The I. B. C. would kill you if I escaped. They'd know about it, all right. Anyhow, there's a risk; and when—her happiness is on it—I'm not going to risk—you."

There was a silence from below the window.

"That's all," said John Arnold, slowly relaxing the cramped muscles that were holding him up to the window. He tautened them again for a last word. "Remember! Look after her—well!"

Under the cell window, recovering from his daze, Grant called and called again; but there was no answer. Inside, Arnold was sitting on his cot again, hands clenched tightly together, lips set into a thin white line.

After a few minutes, which seemed to his strained ears like eternities, he heard the soft pad-pad-pad of a pony's hoofs, receding. And almost immediately, he was asleep.

He slept on, sitting there in the darkness, until ten o'clock in the morning; oblivious and careless of the events, for and against his cause, that were passing under the soft, warm, fragrant tent of that spring night. They were none of his concern, any more. Though, to the outsider, his course of action might appear mysterious; though his actions seemed contradictory; though the character behind those actions might defy analysis—John Arnold, as he slept, was the captain of his soul, with a straight course before him, looking peaceful in comparison with the troubled wake aft.

He did not stir at the moment when his men, hearing of David Grant's fruitless mission, began to gather for a frontal assault on the jail; nor when a coward among them, trembling in his saddle, quoted Arnold's own order that the band should do nothing on his behalf, to get its members into trouble. The coward was knocked senseless by one of his companions; but his advice had delayed action past the moment, when, under the sagacious orders of Mr. William Rigby, a jail guard of a hundred I. B. C. men rode into the square before the prison steps.

Mr. Rigby and the district attorney were having a busy time, furthermore, coaching the witnesses who had appeared before the grand jury. One of them, being drunk, was betraying unsuspected weaknesses of character.

"It's a bunch of damn lies," he was muttering feverishly, "an' suppose we get found out? I won't go back to no jail. I'm out now, an' I'm goin' to stay out!"

"You won't go to jail," said the district attorney soothingly. "You're just telling a straight, truthful story, and—"

"You mean *you* won't go to jail," cried the puncher. "We know that well enough! But us—perjury on a charge of murder—you know what the punishment for that is? You know? It's death, that's what it is!"

"Not in this state," said the district attorney.

Mr. William Rigby cocked an eye at his learned friend.

THE SAGE HEN

"We can't pull him out," whispered the D. A. despairingly, "and we can't delay the trial. It's coming on at ten-thirty, and if the prisoner's ready, we've got to proceed."

Mr. Rigby considered and was cheered.

"After all," he murmured, "it's just a formality—just a formality. He has no counsel, doesn't want any, and pleads guilty. Almost a pity there must be the form of a trial."

The perjurers, their foreman, and their employer, sat for a moment in the lamplight, staring at one another sulkily, fearfully, or thoughtfully, according to their natures. Mr. Rigby was thoughtful.

"Ten years for perjury," he said to the puncher who was drunk, "is better than some other things one could think of. Better than a murder trial on one's own account, for instance. Now, shall we go to bed?"

The drunken puncher was quite sober as they parted, and John Arnold's last chance of salvation through the break-down of the testimony for the prosecution had vanished when that conference broke up; but, knowing nothing of what was happening, and caring nothing about what might be happening, he slept on, undisturbed in mind.

THE SAGE HEN

Mr. Garfield, arriving at ten o'clock to lead him before the bar of the court, was pleasantly surprised.

"Had a good night?" he asked, as he secured Arnold's right wrist to his own brown left.

"Is Miss—Bruce in court?" countered the prisoner.

Mr. Garfield shook his head.

John Arnold started for the door of the cell.

"All right," he said, "then let's go!"

CHAPTER XXI

FROM the cramped confinement of a cell to the comparative freedom of a court room, the change would seem to be for better; but the Hurst County jail was new; while the court-house, across at the other side of the square, dated from the gloomiest days of the 'seventies; and as John Arnold passed out of the brilliant sunshine of the square, under the wooden statue that was labeled "Justice"—lest somebody should mistake it for a cigar store Indian—the cold darkness of the place oppressed him.

All the way from the jail, as old Bill Garfield stumped steadily beside him, the prisoner's level gray eyes had taken in forces arrayed against him; had noted his enemies' precautions against any disturbance of this, the last act of the drama in which he starred. Mounted men with rifles and full gun belts lounged everywhere, smoking and chatting. The court-house square was ablaze with holiday neckcloths and violently checked shirts; the still hot air above it was bluer with tobacco smoke than it was yellow with the dust of arriving reinforcements. The whole scene, on that lovely morning, meant Death for the man who walked through it; yet, even when there descended upon the waiting cohorts the sudden silence that meant they had seen him, and that they knew of his impending fate, the prisoner had felt no sinking of the heart. Out in the sunshine, out in the dust; amid men who carried arms, and in sight of ponies swishing their tails against flies, to-day as on any other day, John Arnold felt at home, and no matter what the actual danger, comparatively safe.

"You're taking good care of my little pony?" he asked Bill Garfield, on the lowest of the court-house steps.

"Sure. Through this door to the right."

They were in the entrance hall of the court, a stuffy cubby-hole smelling of heat-melted brown varnish, tobacco-saturated clothes, and faint carbolic. Now, pushing open a stained-glass door, they passed into a gray dingy corridor across which, at one point, a yellow-paned window threw a bar of

THE SAGE HEN

incongruously cheerful light. A dozen men who had been waiting in the entrance hall followed them, elbowing each other, crowding and staring.

Mr. Garfield turned at the double swung doors of the court room itself, and fumbled for the key of the handcuffs.

"Keep back, there," he said.

The tumblers of the locks clicked. Arnold drew a deep breath. Mr. Garfield eyed him piercingly.

"Feel all right?" he asked.

The prisoner nodded.

"Well, then, good luck," whispered the old man, pushing open the door. "Go in ahead of me."

For an instant, Arnold stood in the doorway alone, blinded, himself, by the obscurity of the court room; conscious that everybody in the packed place was staring at him. In mind, he was calm; in body, confused. He knew that he was expected to make some move, but he could not see the alleyways between the blocks of men who had come to see his finish. His lips tightened; he broke into a fine perspiration.

"Bring the prisoner within the bar," said a thin cold voice from somewhere ahead of him.

Mr. Garfield's bony grip fastened upon his elbow and impelled him forward. The gloom seemed to clear as he moved down what he now saw to be the central aisle of the court. It was pretty light, at that, once one's eyes had grown accustomed to it. There was the judge, in a rusty black gown, leaning forward with arms folded on his desk; there was the jury box; there was the lawyer's table with its surrounding chairs—all empty save two. The thin man standing by one of them was the district attorney. Beside him, Mr. William Rigby sat at ease.

"Sit down," whispered Mr. Garfield.

"Is this the prisoner, Arnold?"

The district attorney rattled some quite unnecessary papers and cleared his throat.

"This, your Honor," he said, "is the prisoner, John Arnold, alias Walter Haynes, charged upon indictment by the grand jury that he did upon the twentieth day of—that is to say, charged with murder in the first degree upon the body of James Bruce."

There was a sickening silence. The judge, wetting a finger, turned over some papers.

"—did with malice aforethought feloniously kill

THE SAGE HEN

and murder," he murmured to himself. "Yes. I understand that this case is ready for trial?"

"The state is ready."

"And the defense?"

Arnold, turned around in his chair, had been looking back into the body of the court.

"And the defense? Is the defense ready to proceed?"

Mr. Garfield nudged the prisoner gently.

"Judge is asking if you're ready for trial," he whispered.

"Yes—"

"Stand up and tell him so, then."

Slowly the big man with the gray eyes rose from his chair.

"I'm ready," he said hoarsely. "Go ahead."

"You are charged with murder in the first degree," said the judge slowly. "How do you plead, John Arnold, guilty or not guilty?"

Every breath in the court room was audible; for suddenly, the half-checked buzz of whispering, the scrape of feet on the floor, the creak of belts, and the rustle of clothing, stopped entirely, leaving an empty silence through which the slightest sound came clearly. Outside, a pony whickered in the heat.

"How do you—" prompted Mr. Garfield; but stopped as the prisoner looked at him. John Arnold's face showed that he had heard the question. The lips were pressed together; the eyes narrowed; the cheeks had suddenly taken on the dampness of the forehead.

"Guilty or not guilty?" droned the judge.

"Guilty!"

There was a hiss of released breath from the watchers in the body of the court.

"I can not accept that plea in a case of this nature," droned the judge unemotionally. "The clerk will enter a plea of not guilty."

Suddenly Arnold chuckled. It seemed rather amusing that the law should require a man to be put through the eternity of agony through which, in the last moment, he had passed, and then take no notice of the result.

This was a fool's game, anyway. Contemptuously he looked at Mr. William Rigby, who seemed to think he was having a private triumph; at the district attorney, who was endeavoring to look like the unwilling servant of the people, performing a duty not at all to his personal taste; and then he turned in his chair again, to look at the crowd behind him.

There, on a long bench by themselves, were the four perfectly strange punchers who had sworn before the grand jury to having been in his company when he had killed James Bruce. One of them appeared to be drunk; all of them became suddenly intent on something else as the gray eyes of the prisoner, smiling mockingly, fastened upon them. The drunkard was otherwise affected. He seemed nervous—rather more than nervous, in fact. He stared back at the victim of his perjury with eyes that showed a rim of white all around the pupil. He was even starting to say something, when Mr. Garfield again touched his prisoner on the arm.

"Judge is askin' you if you don't want counsel," he said.

Arnold rose again.

"No," he said.

"You know that it is your right to challenge any member of the jury we are about to select," said the judge. "Any one whom you may suspect of prejudice or anything like that."

THE SAGE HEN

"Yes."

The judge laid down his pen irritably.

"I should advise you, Arnold," he said, "to pay attention to this case. The charge against you is extremely serious. Don't you know that?"

"Do you think I'm a fool?"

The district attorney gasped.

"I—" he began.

"You shut up," said John Arnold.

He drew a long breath. The gray eyes fixed upon the judge's face and remained there.

"Listen," said the prisoner at the bar; and complete silence fell.

"I'm standing here pleading guilty to a charge of murder, the penalty for which is death. I haven't got anything more than that to say; but I don't want you-all to think I'm a fool. I'm not. I'm doing nothing because there's nothing to do."

Mr. William Rigby nodded his head almost imperceptibly, as though agreeing that this was true, and grieving over the fact.

"However," said John Arnold slowly, "I don't want you gentlemen to kid yourselves. You're going to hang me, and I can't stop you; but I'm going to tell you what you're doing it for—just so you can think about it at night. You're doing it because I took you-all and the International Beef Concern that owns you, and shook justice out of you! One hundred and eighteen thousand dollars' worth."

"This—th-this is beside the point," stammered the district attorney.

"You must confine yourself to the matter in hand," droned the judge. "I have informed you of your right to challenge any member of the jury now to be impanelled."

Arnold laughed. "Amuse yourselves without me," he said, and sat down again.

The court room had seemed large when he entered; now, as he looked around it, the dingy, yellow-plastered walls appeared to have closed in; the stained ceiling with its cheap fake vaulting, to have stooped; the whole place to have grown smaller. And hotter. And stuffier. And more utterly sordid and dull. A man on trial for his life might be supposed to be immune, at any rate, from the affliction of boredom; but John Arnold's heart sank within him under the burden of just this emotion.

"Elmer Magruder," called the clerk.

"Right here!"

"Have you any objection to serving on this jury?"

"Why, no; I guess not."

A pause; then the voice of the district attorney.

"Have you any objection to capital punishment?"

"Capital punishment? Why, no."

"No objection by the state."

"Have you any challenge against this juryman, Arnold?"

The prisoner stared at the talesman; and chuckled again. A regular lowbrow; a typical Beef Concern henchman; standing there trying to look dispassionate, twiddling his Stetson with one hand, and with the other loosening his red neckcloth as if it were a noose about his own throat.

"No, I don't challenge him. I shan't challenge any one. Get ahead with the business."

They got ahead with it; they ran through the curtain raiser to the grand farce in record time, and had the jury gabbingly sworn to well and truly try the issue, and a true verdict give according to the evidence, so help them God, within half an hour.

CHAPTER XXII

OUTSIDE, John Arnold reflected, as the district attorney rushed through his introductory speech and called his first witness to the stand—outside, it was getting on toward high noon; the men in the doorways of the court-house square would be starting to think, and to talk in the leisurely Texas way, of lunch; and (as the champion spoiler of lunches)—of prohibition; and, since they were on the subject of laws, to wonder how the murder trial was going. It seemed queer that they should be free—perfectly at liberty to get on the ponies whose pawings broke the district attorney's drone—and ride anywhere they liked. It seemed strange, too, that he, John Arnold, sitting there so calmly, free so far as bodily bonds were concerned, could not wander even so far as the door by which he had entered; that, after all his years of foot-loose travel over the broad miles of the Southwest, his tracks for the future should be so short—and so plainly marked.

He wrenched his attention back within the walls of the court.

One of the four perjurers was on the stand, looking very uncomfortable and defiant.

"Your name?" asked the district attorney, when the oath had been administered.

"William Slade," mumbled the witness.

"Where were you on——on the twenty-fifth day of July, last year?"

William Slade licked his lips. He had been asked this question before, in the district attorney's office, and had answered it with the truthful word "Arizona." For this slip, he had been so seriously corrected by Mr. William Rigby that the uppermost fact in his mind at the moment was that he must on no account say "Arizona" again.

So naturally, being flustered, he said it; and then, to make matters worse, corrected himself.

"Arizona. No, I mean——I was down here in Texas."

John Arnold laughed.

"You did better than that before the grand jury," he remarked.

"You will not interrupt the witness," said the

judge coldly. "Your turn for cross-examination will come later. Go on, Mr. District Attorney."

But the examiner-in-chief was waiting for his witness to cool down.

"Tell the court," he said at last, "in your own words, what happened on that date."

Mr. Slade licked his lips again, and drew a deep breath. Also, after the immemorial usage of liars, he began to play with his chin, in such a manner that his fingers partly covered his trembling lips.

"Why, I was ridin' with the prisoner there," he remarked, pointing to John Arnold, but not looking at him, "an' suddenly we seen this Bruce boy ridin' toward us, an' Arnold says, 'I got an account to settle with this guy,' an' he rides up to him, an' he shoots him, an' then he kind of goes mad, an' starts cuttin' him up with a knife, an' then afterwards, he takes the body—"

"Are you employed by the International Beef Concern?" snapped the prisoner suddenly.

"No."

"Then what were you doing riding with me that time? It's claimed I killed him because he was fighting the I. B. C. and—"

"Your Honor, I object to this questioning."

"Sustained." The judge scowled at the informal cross-examiner. "You must not interrupt the witness. You may cross-examine him later. You must not interrupt the business of the court."

Arnold laughed.

"Mustn't I?" he asked. "And what'll you do if I choose to go on?"

The judge bit his lip.

"If you are acquitted of this charge," he mumbled, "I will sentence you—for contempt of court."

Arnold rose again; and Mr. Garfield rose with him. But there was no need. The prisoner was not going to leap forward, or throw anything, as men have been known to do when the humors of the law piled up beyond a certain point. Words were all he flung toward the bench; and though they were rather unpleasant words, they justified no violent action on Mr. Garfield's part.

"You old vulture," said the level voice. "Are you trying to deceive *me?* Keep your lying on the witness stand, where it belongs. Don't lie to me."

There was a silence. Then, in rather a faltering voice, the district attorney proceeded.

"Did—James Bruce—attack the prisoner?" he asked.

Mr. Slade's eyes were fixed on those of John Arnold.

"The murder was—entirely unprovoked," he said mechanically.

"What does 'unprovoked' mean?" snapped Arnold. "Quick!"

"Why—er—it means—it means——"

"Ah! You stupid liar!"

"Your Honor!"

Arnold laughed again—laughed loud and long.

"Oh, go ahead," he told the district attorney, "go ahead. I won't interrupt you any more. Bring 'em all on. They'll all say the same thing—in the same words. Go ahead."

Silence.

"You'd do better," quavered the prosecutor, "to bring evidence in rebuttal, if you don't agree with what these men say. Evidence—in rebuttal."

"I haven't had a chance to coach any witnesses," said Arnold. "Go ahead with yours."

"You wished to plead guilty anyhow."

"I pleaded guilty. Yes, and I've cut my own

THE SAGE HEN

hair. But I wouldn't stand for anybody else doing it—by trickery. Go ahead. Your witness is all right again now."

But the district attorney thought otherwise. He distrusted Mr. William Slade at the best of times; and, shaken as the truthful gentleman now was— He glanced quickly at the other witnesses-in-waiting. They were all shaken—visibly so; and while the jury wasn't going to quarrel with their stories, however told, the district attorney had his own professional pride.

He therefore played for time.

"I may say, your Honor," he remarked unctuously, "though it has nothing to do with the case, that the prisoner's suggestion concerning the International Beef Concern is entirely false. The Concern, I am informed, was on the best of terms with young Mr. Bruce, and with his father, at the time of the—"

"I object to this," said Arnold lazily. "It's a lie, and it's beside the point."

The judge ignored him.

"And—and—in short—" stammered the district attorney, "I may say that the International Beef

Concern is in no way implicated in this matter at all."

The judge nodded.

"Have you any other witnesses?" he asked.

"George Carter!" called the prosecutor.

George Carter took the stand.

"Where were you on the twenty-fifth day of July last?"

"With the prisoner, ridin' over beyond the Circle R ranch."

"Tell us what happened."

"I was ridin' with the prisoner there, an' this boy Bruce came ridin' toward us—"

Like a Sunday-school child reciting some horrible piece at a picnic, he told the rest of the story; braced himself for cross-examination, and was permitted to depart unquestioned.

Hughes Evans succeeded him, with the same evidence; used the word "unprovoked"; and sat down, sweating.

The drunken perjurer, who gave his name, first as Hollow Jim, and then as James Holloway, came last, and gave the worst performance. It almost seemed, for a moment, as though he were going to refuse to speak at all; and then, even after he had caught Mr. William Rigby's eye and begun to tremble, he appeared to have forgotten what he had to say.

But somehow, with the aid of leading questions and many pauses, he stumbled through his recitation. It was by the strangest of chances that Arnold, watching him with a grim smile in his eyes, snapped the one question that would hit the witness hardest:

"Do you know the penalty for perjury?"

"No! Damn you, what—"

"I object!"

"Sustained!"

The witness was staring at the prisoner furiously, the white ring around his eyeballs giving him a wild insane look. Arnold appraised it, and spoke soothingly.

"Well, you'd better look out the judge doesn't show you what it is," he murmured, "at the same time he's committing me for—contempt of court."

"That'll do, Holloway!"

"Well, I ain't lyin'! The man who says I am—"

"That'll do! Sit down!"

THE SAGE HEN

Then the district attorney turned to the judge.

"Your Honor," he said deferentially, "that is our case. The state rests."

"Any evidence for the defense?"

"No."

"Very well, Mr. District Attorney," said the judge, laying down his pen and leaning back in his judicial chair. "You may address the jury."

CHAPTER XXIII

THERE was a gasp from the body of the court; and the judge realized, instantly, that in his preoccupation, he had been too hasty. Every man present knew that John Arnold's case was decided—that the verdict had been given and sentence passed, even before he was brought into the court room; but after all, there were certain decencies to be observed. The farce of a trial had gone badly enough so far; half the spectators, having come to rejoice over the fall of a detested enemy, were finding it hard to believe that the casual mumblings, the dull drone of officials, the incoherencies they had just heard, really constituted a function as the result of which the state of Texas might take away a man's life; the other half, realizing it, were not rejoicing to any great extent. With the best will in the world to please Mr. Rigby, whose eyes roamed the court all over and continually, they were feeling rather nauseated. The room was so stuffy. . . . One big puncher rose and opened a window; and leaned out for a moment, breathing deeply.

"But before you address the jury," the judge corrected himself, "I must warn the prisoner that—that—that this is a very serious charge, and that, if he has any witnesses as to his innocence, or as to any extenuating circumstances, or—anything of that nature—he—should call them."

Arnold stared at the man who was to pronounce sentence of death upon him within five minutes. He looked at him for at least thirty seconds of that total of three hundred, and then he smiled. The judge, meantime, had felt a cold dew break out on the palms of his hands.

"I've got no witnesses to call," said John Arnold lazily. "I pleaded guilty. I know what I'm doing. Go ahead."

The judge made a sign.

"May it please your Honor, gentlemen of the jury," began the district attorney. "I—"

He scanned the faces before him in the jury box, and his heart failed him. He was a cruel, brutal and cowardly man; had he not been so, the International Beef Concern would have taken good care he was not district attorney until such time as its business in the county was over. But the most brutal, cowardly and cruel of men are afflicted, in some respects, with the same weaknesses and strengths as the best of us; and the district attorney was finding it extremely difficult to put any real steam into this business. It was too easy. Like his lay brethren in the body of the court, the district attorney, as he faced the jury, became slightly nauseated. He could see, from every face in the jury box, that a verdict of "Guilty!" was ready; that the end of the farce had already come; that everything was over; that the objective laid down by Mr. William Rigby had been achieved; and he felt unable—physically unable—to pretend any more. He felt much like a man who has just beaten an unresisting animal to death; weary, sick and a little frightened. Why did the damned prisoner lounge in his chair so carelessly?

"I scarcely think there is anything I can say to— the jury," said the district attorney weakly. "This man has brought forward no evidence. The state, on the other hand, has shown by four witnesses whose evidence has not been—has not been disputed —that—that—"

THE SAGE HEN

There was a noise outside; there was a rustle in the court; the district attorney paused; and Mr. William Garfield rose to his feet. The noise grew louder; somebody was entering the court building over violent protests of many men in the lobby.

Suddenly, the stained-glass door which led into the dingy corridor crashed open, with a splintering and tingle of broken glass; there were shouts; the sound of running feet in the corridor; the double doors of the court room were flung open.

"I demand to be heard!" shouted a man's voice hysterically. "I demand to be heard!"

With a sudden oath, John Arnold sprang from his chair and, almost before any one in the court room was aware of his movement, had leaped toward the newcomer, hands clutching as if for the man's throat.

This was scope for Mr. Garfield's undoubted abilities as a preserver of decorum in prisoners at the bar. As John Arnold leaped for the new witness, Mr. Garfield leaped for John Arnold, clutched him, twisted sinewy old hands in the prisoner's shirt, thrust a battered peg-leg in the path of his scarcely checked rush, and brought him crashing and fighting to the ground.

THE SAGE HEN

"Lie there, condemn you!"

"Let me up! For God's sake!"

"Jake!" roared Mr. Garfield. "Help! He'll get away from me! Get to the witness stand, you!"

While Mr. Henson assisted his chief to hold down the calm cool prisoner who had so suddenly become maniacal, the new witness stepped forward, not to the stand, but to the bar.

"You—have evidence to give—in this case?" asked the judge, watching the struggle on the floor, and raising his voice above the uproar.

"Yes!"

"What is your name?"

"For God's s——" came the voice of John Arnold, cut off suddenly as Jake Henson clamped a vast leathery hand over his mouth.

A sudden silence fell.

"My name," said the newcomer, in the middle of it, "is James Bruce."

Suddenly, Arnold ceased struggling and lay limp. Jake Henson took the hand away from his mouth. He did not speak, and when he struggled to rise, Mr. Garfield and his deputy assisted him. The sounds thus made were the only noises in court for perhaps five seconds. The judge, pale as a sheet, the district attorney with his papers, Mr. William Rigby, half standing at his place, the jury, the crowd in the body of the court, even the men who had crowded from their post in the lobby into the doorway of the court, stood paralyzed and motionless. The voice of the boy at the bar, though they could hear every syllable distinctly, came to their ears as though from a great distance.

"I am James Bruce of the Circle R. . . . I was not murdered. . . . I ran away . . . I ran away from the fighting. . . ."

His voice broke; he stopped for a moment; then went on more loudly than before:

"This man said he had killed me . . . to save me . . . my family . . . from disgrace."

The district attorney made an attempt to smile cynically and failed.

"When my sister took over the ranch . . . and needed help . . . I let Arnold come back here, at the risk of his life . . . because I was still a coward. . . ."

"Well, you ain't much of a coward now," said Mr. William Garfield, through clenched teeth. "I'll say that."

"I hadn't wanted my father to know, that's how this murder thing started. I didn't want my . . . sister to know, and because I'd once befriended him . . . he risked the murder charge . . . he —came back into this state—to help her."

The silence continued. No one moved. Mr. Garfield noted, for the first time, that Hurst County court room boasted a clock. He could not see it from where he stood, but he could hear its every tick very distinctly.

"How—do we know—this—is true?" asked the district attorney in a cracked voice.

He was not answered in words; the clock ticked on.

"Have you any one here, who—" asked the judge after what seemed an eternity—it was six clock-ticks; Bill Garfield counted them.

"I'll swear to him," Jake Henson rumbled.

"And me," said Mr. Garfield.

But they neither of them did, as it happened; there was no more swearing done at all; though the law demanded quite a considerable amount of it, if the formalities were to be observed.

For Joan Bruce had been looking out of the window of her room in the Hurst Seat Hotel when Jake Henson passed with his companion; and, weeping hysterically, she had followed their gallop, afoot through the streets.

Now she appeared at the door of the court room.

"Jimmy!"

The young man at the bar of the court spun around, and half raised his arms; then, as the girl rushed forward, shrank away from her, covering his face with his hands.

"Don't—touch me!" he cried, in the voice of a wounded animal.

But the girl's arms were around his neck, and she was crying, and she was, cowardice and reformation apart, his little sister whose dolls he had stolen and—and—all that. James Bruce sank down in the chair John Arnold had occupied, and began to sob; while the Sage Hen knelt by, her arms about his bent shoulders, comforting him.

"Well," said John Arnold. "I guess—I'll go."

No one spoke to him; no one looked at him; he was out of the court room before even Mr. Garfield awoke and started after him at the best speed his peg-leg would allow.

"It's all right," gasped the old gentleman, as his late prisoner turned to confront him. "You're all free, bar the formalities. But I thought somebody outside here might plug you by mistake."

The only plugging that was done, however, was inside.

In brief,—when Mr. William Rigby, attempting to relieve the tension of the scene, got up and told the judge—quite unnecessarily—that the International Beef Concern was sorry for any perjury committed by its employees, and that it would give every assistance in the bringing of the malefactors to justice—the drunken puncher took him quite seriously.

And he was sensitive on the point already.

So that, drawing a revolver, he screamed suddenly: "Double cross us, you unprintable blank blank you, eh?"—and shot Mr. William Rigby through the heart.

CHAPTER XXIV

JUST a week later, through the sunshine of a crystally summery day, John Arnold and Mr. William Garfield were riding toward the Mexican border, and save for the thudding shuffle of hoofs in the sand, and the occasional puff as Mr. Garfield blew out some well-chewed portion of his gray whiskers, the silence which had lasted since the two men left Hurst Seat, remained inviolate.

In Mr. Garfield's opinion—and hence the whisker-chewing—it was a funny layout. Arnold had dropped into the Hurst Seat Hotel to say good-by to Joan Bruce and her brother; had stayed nearly an hour, while Mr. Garfield sat on his horse impatiently in the dusty roadway, and had then emerged looking as if, in that hour, he had aged fifty years and been through a severe illness. In spite of which, he had been perfectly cheerful in his good-bys to Sloan, Corliss, and the other Circle R men who had come to shake his hand; perfectly firm and matter-of-fact in his refusal to let the men of his former gang abandon their prospective respectability and follow him wherever he was going; and then—after that—perfectly silent.

"Nice day," said Mr. Garfield tentatively.

"Yeah," said John Arnold.

That was not much of an opening for a really heart-to-heart conversation.

"I'm glad," said the sheriff, after thought, "that you didn't let that bunch of roughnecks come with you. Do you know I've just found out that they and young David Grant were all drawn up in Dead Man's Row like a blasted dragoon regiment, ready to charge the court-house if anything went wrong with your trial? And there was I, sending my deputy—"

"Yes," said John Arnold, looking steadily ahead into the heat haze. "I know. Thanks."

"Well, of course," said Mr. Garfield vaguely, "I was bound to bring out all the evidence in the case."

He swallowed.

"Say," he demanded, suddenly throwing strategy to the four winds, "how come you're leaving town this way, my boy?"

THE SAGE HEN

With a convulsive movement, Arnold reined in his pony. With a gentle pull on the bridle, and a consolatory clucking of the tongue, Mr. Garfield did likewise.

"I said I was going," Arnold answered hoarsely. "I said I was going—a week ago. Didn't I?"

"But a lot can happen in a week."

"Well?"

"We-eeelll," said Mr. Garfield, staring ahead to where, like a gallows against the sky-line, there showed the international boundary post at Prairie Dog. "Well, I thought a lot *had* happened. I— didn't think you'd be leaving our midst. . . . Look here, my boy. I'm an old man; it looks as if, from now on, for some time, anyhow, I shall have two counties to look after instead of one. Don't leave me puzzling. I can see through a brick wall as far as most men—but no further. Why are you hopping off like this? I mean, what's the big idea?"

John Arnold's eyes, older in their expression than when he had come to Three Pines, considered the wise old face of the sheriff for thirty seconds.

"Why," he said at last, "because I've nothing further to do here, Mr. Garfield; I'm through.

THE SAGE HEN

I've done the work I came to do, the work I'm fit for; an' I'm going before—I make a failure trying to do something else."

"Is that," asked Mr. Garfield, "what you were talking about in the Hurst Seat Hotel?"

"Yes!"

The sheriff took a large mouthful of whisker, and bit it severely.

"How did you phrase it, if I may ask?"

Little drops of perspiration were beading John Arnold's forehead.

"I said that—just because—a bad man—fought in a good cause—that didn't make him—any the less— a bad man. I said a soldier might be a fine soldier —and yet—a rotten—parson. And I said that—in spite of all the stories an' things—a bad man'd better stick—to his place in the world."

"I write stories myself, sometimes," said Mr. Garfield thoughtfully. "It's surprising how much truth you can get into 'em—if you try."

The men's eyes met.

"What else did you say?" asked the old man. "She didn't let you go—just for that?"

Silently, Arnold raised his left hand and held it

out toward the sheriff. On the third finger there gleamed dully a heavy yellow ring. Mr. Garfield drew a sharp sudden breath.

"I never noticed that before," he said.

"Do you now?"

"Why, yes," said the old man slowly. "Now I do, of course. Well—"

And, with their guardian cloud of dust following them as before, the ponies, touched by the spur, ambled forward again. Again, too, there descended upon the cavalcade the silence which had marked its earlier progress and which, this time, endured until the two parties to it stopped at the international boundary post, with the Rio Grande sparkling before them, a gracious foreground to the wilderness of scrub, sand and cactus of the Mexican side.

"Well—" began Arnold, taking one hand off the bridle.

"Is she over there?" asked Mr. Garfield. He spoke rather indistinctly, for the reason that he had added to his first chew of whisker, taken from the right-hand side of his face, another chew bent inward from the left. This was a well-known sign of agitation.

THE SAGE HEN

"Who?"

"Mrs. Arnold."

The tall man looked once at the river, then backward at the hard-bitten landscape of Three Pines County; and finally, straight at Mr. Garfield, who returned the gaze.

"What makes you think I'm married?" he asked mockingly.

Carefully, the sheriff returned his whiskers to their usual position, and settled himself a little lower in his saddle. He also sighed—imperceptibly, almost, but he sighed.

"You're wearing a wedding ring," he said. "They usually give a wife away with one of those."

"Yes," said John Arnold, "I believe they do."

"Well?"

The big man burst out with a strange fury.

"Well, you old fool," he cried. "Do you think I'm not human? Do you think I don't want—to stay here? Do you think I want to go back to the desert and the one-man life? No! And I know just how strong I am—and how weak. I know all about how bad men reform an' make good husbands for good women. She ought to marry David Grant."

THE SAGE HEN

"The only objection being," said Mr. Garfield softly, "that she ain't in love with him. Whereas with you—she is."

"That's enough," whispered Arnold hoarsely.

"As for the bad man turning away from his wickedness—well—I've seen it done."

"That's enough. You won't see it done—this time."

A cottontail scuttered across the path, a little cloud of dust following his busy heels; a big black bird flopped heavily away overhead, with a forlorn cry. Mr. Garfield examined the movements of both with interest, and then sighed gently.

"All the same, it's funny," said he at last, "that you should carry a wedding ring in your war sack, so handy, like."

With a chuckle that was most unpleasant to hear, Arnold raised his hand again—and turned it over. On the underside of the broad gold band which encircled his finger was a small soldered loop.

"They've got a lot of these—in the hall of the hotel," he said breathlessly; and then, with a sudden wrench, tore at the encircled finger and hurled the curtain ring skittering into the dust.

THE SAGE HEN

As if the signal had been prearranged, his pony took one step forward.

So did Mr. Garfield's; and, all of a sudden, the aged sheriff leaned forward in the saddle. Without the slightest shadow of legal justification, but with a lightning expertness which indicated many, many years' experience with the more practical demonstrations of the law, he caught both John Arnold's wrists, and with a flash of polished steel, handcuffed them together. In one and the same motion, it seemed, he also caught the bridle of his prisoner's pony, and wrenched that animal to a halt.

"Wedding rings, eh?" gasped the old gentleman indignantly, settling his hat and staring at his prisoner. "Curtain rings, eh? Can't reform, eh? Broken hearts, eh?"

With another pull at Arnold's bridle, and an application of his peg-leg, clublike, to his own horse's ribs, he revolved the beasts until they faced once more in the direction of Three Pines.

"I've got this business in charge from now on," said Mr. William Garfield cheerfully. "You and your curtain rings! You come on back!"

THE END

Please return when through